stories

MARK BRENDLE

stories
by Mark Brendle

@brendlewhat

Cover photo is a public domain picture of wet cardboard.
For more information about wet cardboard, visit your local
library.

PUBLISHED BY
BRENDLEWORDS
Copyright © 2014 Mark Brendle
All rights reserved.
ISBN: 0988254328
ISBN-13: 978-0988254329

STORIES

THREADBARE

0

It comes into the world with a fundamental scream. It clutches and grasps at the intangible threads of a collapsed non-existence. Its eyes blink open slowly, rapidly, asynchronously. The visible spectrum of light permeates the visible. It wrenches its neck wildly. There is no understanding, just the overcast-light nimbus, the unknowable loss, the inevitable acceptance, the gaping, abject silence. It comes into the world.

The unspeakable sinks down into the inaccessible depths, only rising to the fore in dreams and madness. The conscious interpretation of impulse fails, always fails, and the corrupted translation of an archaic inscription flees the throat with furtive awareness and lands upon the foreign and the strange and is taken for that which it is not. The blame of folly shouldered both by flailing tongues and wanton ears in the perennial carnival of symbolic relation.

The spheres are mirrored, liquid yet impermeable. They collide with the infinitesimal separation of repulsive electron cloud layers, the thin atmospheres repelling endlessly all contact. If they did not, matter would slide through matter and there would be no whatness of any thing, no separation, no dichotomy, only the sliding of this through that, the same fabric forever rewound into itself without pattern or reason. That is no way to live.

1

-Peter, come up.

-Peter, come up and join us.

-Peter, come up and join us.

-What are you doing, Peter?

-What are you doing down there by yourself? Peter?

-Come up, Peter.

Come up.

Hands reaching down, out, grasping. Fingers curling, multi-jointed fingers curling with intention, reaching down, touching, taking. I am Peter.

-Mother, why am I Peter?

-You were named after your father.

-Yes, but why?

-Because. Because.

I felt my body and knew it was mine. I floated on downturned sheets and above rails and went out through myself, through the ceiling, and knew it was mine. I lay and look down at my toes and wiggle them, looking at them, calling them mine, wiggling them, looking at them wiggle, consciously wiggling them, sending the impulse to wiggle. But I think "Toes, wiggle." and they do not. I cannot think them to action. I cannot command them to wiggle. But I wiggle them and they wiggle as I will, not upon the thought, but upon something else, subterranean, dark and secret, inaccessible to this voice of blackness, these eyes of light. But they do wiggle. I lay and watch them, knowing they are mine, that it is I who wiggle, yet cannot think "wiggle" and make it so.

Sometimes I go down there. It is there, so I go. In the muddy, pungent depths. Down, step by step, down the old folding ladder, down into it. There is a black tarp laid over the floor. Beneath the tarp, I assume, is earth, heaving and rippling with the life of the earth, the primordial energy of the many worms and beetles and spiders, burrowing blindly through the soil, digging down further into the warmth and compression, or climbing up, breaking through, sticking out into the muddy air and feeling the terrible freedom of unrestricted passage. But always rippling, always heaving, always alive.

-You could have been thrown in a river.
-Why would I have been thrown in a river, father?
-You know what I gave up for you? You know what I've sacrificed for you?
-Why a river?
-So you'd sink. You could have sunk. I could have tied you in a potato sack and thrown you out of the car window and nobody would have known. You couldn't have helped it. You would have struggled at first, but eventually grown tired. I could have tossed a potato sack out of the car window, driving at a leisurely pace, thrown it right out and into a river.
-Why would you have thrown me? Why?
-You're more trouble than you're worth.
-Am I so much trouble?
-You and your mother both. If I could dump the both of you in a river and just keep driving at a leisurely pace. If I could, you better believe it. You don't even know how good you got it. You have no idea what it's like out there.
-You wouldn't throw mother into a river.
-You better believe it. Just keep on driving. Get me a couple of

potato sacks and take a nice leisurely drive.
-But you wouldn't.
-Just keep on driving, he said.

2

When he came out of me he came out of me he came out of me
to think that he came out of me a part of me made of me of all I
ate and drank and was and when he came out of me like a
bursting like an amputation and I felt the vacuum of his loss and
the hollow he left for me and the blood on the sheets and on
the floor and his crying and crying and crying and screaming and
constantly wanting wanting still taking from my body all I had
and all I was and feeding from me but now outside of me now
other than me now this thing I see and feel and hear always
hear and when I said to his father when I said to him to just put
it in the trash can let's just put it in the trash can and walk away
and erase all the crying and screaming and loss and hollow but I
didn't mean it sweet sweet I didn't mean it no I never meant it
but oh sweet one I never meant it no.

He wouldn't stop crying and we tried everything and even his
father was worried even he knew something was wrong and we
could see it in his face and we didn't know what to do we just
didn't know it wasn't our fault it wasn't how could we know
what he wanted when he just screamed and screamed with his
little hands clutching around him and I was crying and begging
and just wanted it all to stop and we did everything we could
and then when he was better all I could think was that I could
lose him anytime that I walked this tightrope of attachment that
any small thing could sever and I picked him up and held him
close to me and promised that nothing would ever happen ever

again and I would always be there to take care of him because of the shaking in my hands when he was so bad and I felt again that loss of the him in the outside of me and the regret of ever letting go no I never should have let go I never should have cut that tie and the scissors in the blood so sharp so quick like nothing ever mattered again and he cut it and we were ever more not one just two not part of me but like everything else outside of me and when he cried I didn't know what to do how could I?

He's down in there again by himself and I don't know how he keeps getting down there because I told his father to keep it locked and I know he has even though he gritched about it when I told him but I know he would do it because he wouldn't ever want to hurt Peter that I am sure of at least no matter what he says but still I find him down in there in that dirty pit just down there and what is he doing I don't understand him and I haven't understood him since he became he and no longer me but he's down there by himself and I worry for him so I do I am so worried and I wonder if he knows how it makes me feel when he goes off like that if he ever considers my feelings if he ever considers anything but himself like when I walked in on him doing it and the look on his face and the red hot in mine and the image of him doing it even though I thought he must at his age and even though I know they do it to have seen it now and he's just another man just a small man soon to be like the others like all the others taking what they can with that thing they have and he'll never once consider how I feel because I do feel I do I have feelings and when he climbs down in there I just break and scatter I just lacerate and spill I just burst and burst with the same agony of our first separation.

3

THIS IS HOW YOU HOLD A FISHING ROD.
THE ANGLE THE WRISTS ARE VERY IMPORTANT.
YOU HOOK THE WORM.
YOU PIERCE IT.
IT WRIGGLES IN YOUR FINGERS.
I WANT TO TEACH YOU HOW TO FISH.
GET A WORM.
GET A FUCKING WORM.
PUT YOUR FUCKING HAND IN THE BUCKET AND GET A WORM.

The worm wriggles in his fingers and he's crying and not looking at it like a little baby and just holding it out as far as he can from his body, holding it with just the very tips of his fingers.

SHE MADE HIM LIKE THIS.
SHE DRIVES A WEDGE.
SHE RUINS EVERYTHING.

Her and her fucking bullshit.

JUST PUT THE FUCKING WORM ON THE HOOK.

He's crying and holding it out. Like it's going to eat him. A worm. I show him. I've showed him now a bunch. He won't do it.

-No, that's all right. It's all right.
[YOU PUSSY]
-You don't have to fish, Peter.
[YOU LITTLE FAGGOT]
-It's not for everyone.

-It's all right son. It's all all right.

4

After the storm, I go to the tree. The tree in our yard. It has no
leaves. It smells like rain all around and I can see the earth like a
fresh grave turning up its secrets. There are worms in the soil.
They crawl and flop across leaves, needles and dirt. The sick,
slimy contraction and expansion of their bodies. Like the worm
corpse in Biology with the formaldehyde stink, slowly split up
the middle with little white parts and little black parts and
strings and bulbous clumps and rubbery skin. What was dead is
now alive.

To find, beneath the black tarp, the churning of life. In the soil.
Down there, down the ladder, in the soil. To find it churning.
The movement of many legs over my body like pinpricks
teasing. Returning, descending down, returning home. I can
hold my hands out to the side and feel them go to sleep, my
fingers spread out, waning into the blackness. I can feel them
slip away. I can look at them like they don't belong to me. I can
see them as part of this soil, remote from me. My sleeping
hands descending into the soil, wet and dirty, absent and
remote. I can hold my arms out. I can slowly dismember myself
piece by piece, each sleeping, sleeping, as I descend. Until I am
all eyes. Until the sound drowns out. Until the submersion.
Down, down, down.

A shadow hunkers over the door, squatting low. It's all
silhouette, all black. I'm lying on my back, down here. Not
moving.

-Peter, come up and join us.

I say nothing. I do not move. The frequency of the soil rumbles in my ears and I hear it speaking to me out of the void. I see my hands from afar. I see my toes. I see.

-What are you doing, Peter?

In the dirt under my nails. In the ripping off of nails and the pulling out of hair. Of all these dead things. She sways, slowly, back and forth, back and forth, eating the light.

-What are you doing down there, by yourself?

Or our teeth. Grinding and grinding and grinding. Eroding. Not in the soil, in the soil, breathing the soil, feeling the soil. Truncated by suffocating earth. Filling the mouths of existence. Filling the holes. All the while wriggling and rumbling and undulating with life. Always.

-Come up, Peter.

The threads I've torn from my skin, pulled out like a handmade doll. Button eyes falling apart. Staring, empty, out, across. All these threads I've torn. Empty staring at my threadbare being. Pulling out all the threads until I sink and descend to the final return. Falling to pieces. My hands sleep. My pieces sleep. I inventory them and tally them and pull at the threads that stitch me together. See how I rend me? Piecemeal me? The earth pulling down on my back. The death inside me pushing down on my chest. My empty staring, upwards and out, beyond, limitless and luminous. Shed these tattered fragments of soil. Erase this latticework awareness. Sleep, hands. Sleep and descend. Down, down, down. To the final return.

- Come up.

ART SCHOOL

A single flower sits in a small, clear vase on the window sill in the kitchen. She picked it from her yard. She gardens, is a garden dilettante, out in the yard during the day, when the sun shines and her husband is at work in a building just outside downtown. She picked the flower herself. She brings the outside inside. She wants beauty to be by her as she moves through her day. She arranges it just so, facing it the right direction so it catches the light in a certain way at a certain time of day, when the window blinds are adjusted to a specific angle and the whole kitchen is bathed in the diffused afternoon. She stops and smells the flower. She has the time to stop and smell it. It smells good.

She eats a quiet breakfast of granola and yogurt in her husband's favorite chair. The television is off. Early on cold mornings, when the roofs are frosted over and the whole landscape glints, before the mid-morning sun melts it away, she turns on the gas fireplace and watches it dance between spoonfuls. If he left any coffee in the pot, she pours herself a cup. Occasionally she will brew a new cup when the pot is empty, but not usually. She takes milk in her coffee and a packet of artificial sweetener.

The shows she likes to watch come on and she sits down to watch them, petting the cat if he comes within petting distance. Her cat's name is Magritte. She knows the shows she watches are silly and part of her enjoyment in watching them comes from laughing at their silliness. But still she watches them, sometimes surprising herself with an emotional response to some cliché plot line or character arc. She reminds herself to see them for what they are.

Many years ago, before she got married the first time, she studied art history. She pored over the impressionists, the surrealists, the neo-realists, memorized their details, could easily distinguish a painting she had never seen before by school and sometimes by artist. She never put paint to canvas herself, but had a great respect for those who did. She admired the grace of a brush stroke, the curve of a back, or the angle of a tilted head. She loves Picasso. She loves vibrant reds and golds. She remembers how a Pollack exploded its energy and how a Rothko bottled the energy up within tight geometry.

When her shows are over, she begins her work. She starts with the dusting, wiping off each flat surface with a cloth, collecting each dust particle in her hand, each sliver of disuse, all evidence of the untouched, unchanging stillness until it all looks new, pristine and new, without a trace of time's indifferent blanket. Then onto the polish. She shines each piece of furniture until it gleams. The polish is hard on her hands, but she rubs the wood and leather thoroughly with their respective polishes and when she is done, she washes her hands in the sink with a special moisturizing hand soap she found at the grocery store.

From there, she moves on to vacuuming. She methodically runs the vacuum cleaner in familiar patterns over the carpet, stopping to move furniture or return a cat toy to its bucket. Magritte oscillates between fear and curiosity, suspiciously eying the vacuum from a safe distance. She knows the patterns well and her arm pushes and pulls automatically as her mind wanders. Her favorite painter was de Chirico and she remembers being haunted in her youth by his empty agoras, solitary gazing statues, and shadows lengthened by an impossible sun. One painting she recalls particularly, that of a headless, limbless, truncated statue of a female body sunbathing next to a pile of ripe bananas on a stone dais in the foreground, while a series of hollow arches drag into the background where a brick wall obscures the passing of a distant train, its smokestack echoing cloudy trails across the sky. She enjoys the feeling of a freshly vacuumed carpet under her feet. Of late she's taken to wearing slippers in the house, but she always removes them and walks gently across the living room when her vacuuming is done. She's careful to put all the furniture back in its place, setting each chair and table leg into its divot. She imagines all the dirt pulled up from the carpet whizzing through the intricate tubes of the vacuum, and watches the hairy clumps tumble out from the receptacle as she empties it into the trash. She's careful not to get dust on her clothes as she ties the handles of the trash bag together and takes it into the big trash bin in the garage.

She takes her lunch on the back porch. Her house sits atop a hill and she looks out across the neighborhood, beyond to the farms and the vineyards, and beyond to the tree covered mountains. Magritte now blissfully lounges in his cat bed. Her lunch consists of a turkey sandwich, dry, with a carrot. She drinks water with her lunch, never indulging in a glass of wine during the day. She has one with dinner sometimes, but gave up drinking before dinner years ago. She enjoys sitting outside when the weather is nice and all is quiet except perhaps for the sound of neighbors working on their yard, or the hum of heavy farm machinery, which sometimes kicks up dust clouds large enough to see. The view from her house is beautiful, the main reason she wanted the house. Her husband agreed, but rarely sets foot on the unstained deck anymore. Sometimes a glint in the mountains will catch her eye, a beam of sunlight reflected off of the window or antenna of some far away house on another hill and she wonders if someone else can see a gleam from her direction. She takes care not to stay too long outside. A few minutes with an empty plate and she returns indoors without a final look at the neighborhood, the farmland, the vineyards, or the tree covered mountains.

After lunch she begins the dishes. Most of her dishes came as wedding gifts. Some were her mother's. Others were purchased on short vacations. She washes each dish by hand before setting it in the dishwasher, scrubbing it with the brush under a stream of hot water until she's satisfied, then placing it in the dishwasher carefully. Each dish, or type of dish, has a specific place in the dishwasher. She has learned through trial and error how to most effectively arrange the dishes. As she washes a heavy, white plate she is reminded of a Lichtenstein that shows a blonde lying on a bed with gold rails, shooting an angry look at an alarm clock. She remembers how the yellow of the blonde's hair flows into the bed rail on one side and into the alarm clock on the other. The comic image, blown up to ridiculous proportion, each dot visible, reveals the truth of its make-up and color. That is how she drops the plate, losing focus, thinking on this painting from her past. The plate falls quickly, hitting the wood floor of the kitchen on its side, shattering into several large shards and many smaller ones. She gasps and steps backward. Magritte leaps in alarm.

She steps back at first, recoiling from the noise and the violent motion. Instinctively, she begins to tip-toe through the pieces, glad to be wearing slippers, and moves towards the dustpan and brush. She turns back to the shattered plate, already kneeling to clean it up, when the sun filters through the blinds in the kitchen window and strikes the flower in its vase and continues down onto the floor where it is reflected off the scattered shards. She sinks to her knees, but drops the dustpan and brush beside her. She gazes motionless, the hardwood pressing painfully against her kneecaps. She begins to cry.

Her chest swells with laborious sobs and she cries viciously for several minutes. The fragments of the plate remain inert on the floor, glinting with sunlight. The dishwasher door hangs open, the bottom rack pulled out, half full, dripping water into the tray. When she gathers herself, all is quiet. She looks again at the broken dish and suddenly stands up. She walks to the kitchen table and takes a bunch of bananas from the fruit dish. She sets them down among the shards of plate and sits back down on the floor. She smiles, then laughs. She laughs out loud. Magritte tilts his head to one side. She laughs again, admiring, basking, reveling in her scene. She quiets and rests. She sits comfortably on the floor, her back against the cabinets. Here she watches as the shadow of the window blinds slowly moves across the floor, until finally the light changes and repeals its magic.

She stands up, grabs the bananas, and places them back in the fruit dish. She bends over carefully, takes the dustpan in her left hand, the brush in her right, and systematically cleans up the plate. She empties the dustpan into the trash. Even though the trash bag is otherwise empty, she ties it up and takes it out into the garage. She puts a new bag in the bin. She finishes the dishes in the waning daylight and glances at the clock regularly.

She hurries up the stairs and enters the bathroom. She splashes water onto her face. It feels cool and refreshing. She washes off her makeup, takes a quick glance at her natural face, her brown eyes, her thin eyebrows, her slightly sagging cheeks. She re-applies her makeup. This too she does precisely, automatically, until she looks just so.

She hears the garage door open just as she finishes. She hurries back down the stairs, careful not to trip over Magritte, who winds his way in and out of her path. She stands before the door to the garage, calming herself, slowing her heart rate. Her soul swells with pensive anticipation, reminding her of Hopper's Hotel Room, just as the door opens and he walks in.

He smiles at her and removes his coat. They kiss briefly on the lips. His face is haggard and his eyes are red and tired. His shoulders sit with a familiar slump.

"Welcome home," she says.
"Hi baby," he says.
"How was your day?" she asks.
"Long," he says. "I'm beat."

He does not ask about her day. She hangs his coat in the closet. He sits down in his favorite chair and removes his shoes. He rubs his temples and eyes. She stands by him. Magritte prances over and rubs against his leg and sniffs his shoes.

"Hey Mags," he says. "How are you, old boy?" he pets the cat on the neck and ears. It purrs at him, circles, and rests near his feet. She takes his shoes and puts them in the closet.

"What's for dinner, sweetie?" he asks. She closes the door to the closet, but does not turn to face him.

"What would you like?" she says. "We can have anything you like."

SHEAR

1

I sweep. I sweep the hair. I sweep the hair he cuts. I sweep the hair he cuts off the floor. I have this broom. There's a radio. Sometimes the radio is on. Sometimes not. I sweep with this broom. The radio can play music. The radio can play the news. The hair piles up on the floor. I sweep it. The man cuts the hair. The man who cuts the hair. The man who cuts the hair's name is uh. The man who cuts the hair, his name is uh. The man who cuts the hair, his name is Frank. I sweep the hair. The radio is off. Frank turns the radio off. When the radio is on, Frank has turned it on. Frank cuts the hair. Frank turns the radio on and Frank turns the radio off. I sweep the hair.

There are chairs. There are two chairs. The men sit in the chairs. The men have many names. The men with many names sit in the chairs and their hair is cut. Frank cuts their hair. Sometimes the other one cuts the hair. His name is uh. The other one who cuts the hair sometimes, other than Frank, his name is uh. Two people can sit in the two chairs. Two people can have their hair cut. Frank can only cut one man's hair at a time. When the other, uh. When the other, uh. When the other one isn't there, only one chair has a man. Sometimes Frank turns on the radio.

A man will sit in the chair. Frank will say something. He will say uh. He will say uh. He will say things. Sometimes Frank turns on the radio. I sweep up the hair. Sometimes Frank says things. Sometimes Frank turns on the radio. I sweep the hair. Frank does not talk to me. Frank has a guitar. Frank's guitar is old. Frank's radio is old. Frank is old. The chairs are old. The men in the chairs are old.

Frank has the scissors. Frank holds the scissors. The scissors. The scissors are. The scissors are sharp. The scissors are sharp and they cut. Frank says uh. Frank says uh. Frank says don't uh. Don't touch. Don't touch the scissors. They cut the hair. I sweep the hair. Frank, using the scissors, cuts the hair. I sweep the hair. I use my broom. I, using my broom, sweep the hair that Frank cuts, using the scissors, off the floor. The floor is old.

There is a bowl. The bowl sits on a table. There is a table. The table is next to a bench. There is a bench. The bench is where the men sit. They sit on the bench before they sit in the chairs. In the bowl, on the table next to the bench where the men sit before they sit in the chairs, is candy. I like the candy. Frank does not like the candy. Frank refills the candy dish. I have seen it. I have seen him. I have seen him refill the candy dish. Sometimes the men take the candy. Sometimes the men eat the candy. Sometimes I take the candy. Sometimes I eat the candy. Sometimes Frank says uh. Sometimes Frank says uh. Sometimes Frank says I better not eat too much.

Frank plays the guitar. Sometimes. Sometimes Frank plays the guitar. When there are no men. When there are no men on the bench or in the chairs, sometimes, Frank plays his guitar. Frank doesn't talk to me. I sweep the hair. Frank plays his guitar. I like Frank's guitar. I do not play Frank's guitar.

The broom is old. The bottom of the broom is old. I clean the bottom of the broom. The hair falls out of the bottom of the broom. I watch the hair fall out of the bottom of the broom. My grip on the broom is tight. I hold the broom tight. I hold on to the broom. I do not drop the broom.

I have three shirts. I wear three shirts. I will wear three shirts. I have a blue shirt. I have a white shirt. I have a red shirt. I will wear the blue shirt. I will wear the white shirt. I will wear the red shirt. Today I wear the red shirt. Frank has many shirts. Frank has a lot of shirts. The men wear different shirts. Everybody has a shirt. The hair gets on my shirt. The hair Frank cuts gets on my shirt. I wipe the hair off my shirt. I sweep the hair off the floor.

When it gets dark. When it gets dark. When it gets dark outside the men go home. I sweep the most when the men go home, when it gets dark. After it gets dark, after I sweep the most, I go home. I do not live at Frank's. Frank does not live at Frank's. There's uh. There's uh. That's the uh. There's. After it gets dark, there's that. And that's the.

2
One of the men has a dog. The dog. What? That dog that. The dog is on the floor. The dog is old. The man with the dog is old. The man with the dog says something. I can't. I don't. The man with the dog says something. Frank says something. I can't. I don't. The thing is. The thing IS. It is. I. The dog has a long tongue. The dog wags his long tongue. The thing is. The dog lays on the floor. Look. I sweep the hair. The man still says. Frank still says. I can't. I don't. The thing is. I sweep the hair. Off the floor. Frank says. I sweep the hair. The man with dog says. Off the floor.

The piles and piles. The piles of hair. Piles and piles. I sweep the hair into piles. I sweep the hair off the floor into piles. I sweep the hair off the floor into piles on the floor. The piles of hair I sweep on the floor. Off the floor. The piles. I sweep. The broom pushes the hair. The hair is from the men. The men sit in the chairs. Frank cuts the hair. The hair falls. I've seen it. I've seen the hair fall. I've swept the hair. I've swept the hair that's fallen. Swept it into the piles. There are piles and piles. The men come in. The men leave. The men come in. Frank cuts the hair. The men leave. They come. The scissors. Frank with the scissors. They leave. The men leave. The men were cut. The men were cut. The men were cut.

Frank says uh. Frank says uh. I can't. I don't. The thing is. THE THING IS. Frank has the scissors. I have the broom. Frank has the radio. Frank turns the radio on. Sometimes. Frank has the guitar. Frank plays the guitar. Sometimes. The radio, the guitar, the scissors. The bench, the chairs, the hair not cut. The broom, the hair cut. There are things. Frank says things. Sometimes. He says uh. The thing is.
Frank has the razor. Sometimes. I've seen the razor. I've seen it. The men. Some men. They sit in the chairs. Frank uses the razor. Frank cuts with the razor. Frank keeps the razor in his pocket. I've seen it. I'm not to touch the razor. There are. There are things. There are things I remember. Don't touch the razor. I've seen it. I've seen Frank. He says uh. He says. The thing is. I. Frank sharpens the razor. Frank has a strap. The strap is brown. The strap. He touches the razor to the strap. He slides the razor across the strap. He runs the razor back and forth back and forth against the strap. It sounds. He folds the razor. He puts it in his pocket. I do not have pockets.

3

I am. I am trying. I am trying to. I am trying to tell. I am trying to tell you. I am trying to tell you something. What it is. What it is. It is. What it is. I. The thing is. I've heard. Frank says uh. Look.

I sweep the hair that he cuts off the floor.
I SWEEP the hair that he cuts off the floor.
I SWEEP THE HAIR that he cuts off the floor.

He cuts. He cuts. He cuts the hair. I sweep the hair. I am trying. He cuts. The thing is. I. LOOK. He cuts. I am trying. The hair. Off the floor. Look. What the thing. Is I. What it LOOK. The thing is. I remember things. He says. He says. Uh. Uh.

Uh. LOOK. The thing is, uh.

I SWEEP THE HAIR THAT HE cuts off the floor.
I SWEEP THE HAIR THAT HE CUTS off the floor.
I SWEEP THE HAIR THAT HE CUTS OFF the floor.
The floor the floor. Look.

I am trying to.

Look. The thing is. Uh. He cuts. The thing IS. He cuts. THE THING IS. He cuts. HE CUTS. HE CUTS.

Frank has said. Uh. Frank has said. Uh. I am trying. LOOK. The thing is. He cuts.

I SWEEP THE HAIR THAT HE CUTS OFF THE FLOOR.
I SWEEP THE HAIR THAT HE CUTS OFF THE FLOOR.
I SWEEP THE HAIR THAT HE CUTS OFF THE FLOOR.

SWEET POTATO PANCAKES

JAMES YOUR FATHER IS DEAD

It's like that, the day after it happens.

But before that voice, a few minutes between sleep and awareness when it's like it hasn't even happened at all. When I can't even think of what it was. Like it never happened.

But it did. That's what you realize after you hear it. That waking up the day after is just a continuance of the day before and not a discrete time or space, no matter how much you might want it to be.

When you're out
When you're out hunting
Haven't been out in a while.
When you're out hunting,
If you slip a bit and maybe don't get a kill shot, but
You don't get a kill shot. A kill shot. But it's dying all the same, only slow and painful. The blood seeps out from a narrow wound and trickles down onto the rocks, the twigs and needles, it trickles out onto the forest floor and, like all blood, cries out to you. It trickles out and cries out. Into the dirt. With the rocks and the twigs and the needles.

And it cries out.

I went hunting with him. My father. I went hunting with him a long time ago. I been a lot since, and you have to. You have to put it down. If you're out hunting and you don't get a kill shot, you know it's dying all the same and you have to put it down and then it's what's called a mercy killing because you're taking away the pain it's in, but you put that pain inside it to begin with.

I move the pain around. I take it out of me. I put it into it. I take the pain and put it inside it and then mercy kill it and kill the pain and put it down because I didn't get that kill shot and when you're out hunting, (it has been a while) you might slip a bit.

Things are sliding away now and I was always worried my mind would be the first thing to slip. Things are sliding away now, things, not my mind. My mind is here and unslipped and settled and aware and how unfortunate that is. But of all the things that slip away I never thought I'd lose them.

Because how can love slip away?

You. To you. Cries out to you. Blood cries out to you. All blood cries out to you. The blood of this wound, festering for almost 20 years now and finally dragging the corpse to the sawbones to amputate the gangrenous sores that have attached to the quick. An amputation nonetheless and now, what with him gone (he is gone), now it's even more on my own and my very own mother grieving with a loss I can't even fathom, for obviously I never knew love like theirs, which blossomed even in late decay, whereas my own has slid out in all directions from my center, while I am only now fading from my prime. Yes, she will grieve and I reckon will not last long. Not without him. Because they knew love and that is the price you pay for love, Lord knows, not me, I will probably live through this, though my ears may shatter from the crying of the blood from the soil and not from my own amputation which, when cut off, will ooze forth only bile and pitch, for all the blood burned out twenty years ago and it's been cold and inert since, but still hanging on, still hanging on and she will grieve and soon be gone and then we will grieve and also soon be gone, but first we get the gangrene cut, because once it festers it poisons the whole.

I never knew love like theirs.

It is gone though, whatever used to be there. I'm not one to try and say, after the fact, that a thing never was, when I would have sworn just the same that it was, when it was, but once it isn't, that don't mean it wasn't and I won't say that, no matter how much hate fills up my heart or Evelyn's, but maybe it wasn't the same, it was a love, but maybe not Love with a capital L, but it was something that most people would take for love and I don't know how the word fits in, but I'm too old for that now and just want to feel what I felt, whatever it was, when I was with and not without and even our girls are going to get hurt in this whole process and there will be much crying and much slipping and if you're out hunting and you don't get a kill shot you can see the blood trickle onto the floor of the forest and with a second shot you can deliver mercy unto a

(Tonight, I will read the gospels.)

When I moved away from all the noise and the dirt (this is a dirty dirt, a grime, a film, another time my lack of gift with words leaves me blank, but a something far worse than the dust

of the soil and the pungent manure) when I moved away from
the city, with the traffic and the suits and the rush and the quick
and the little lighted hubs of humanity that are only so
important when you're in it and can't see out like the fish in the
ocean swimming around in circles, or maybe a fish tank, and
they can see out but can't process the information, I mean even
if it were people and not fish. I'm trying to say, when I moved
away from all that, I thought I would find my peace. But (I've
had a history of hunting) it's not to be found, even out here. I
could describe my ranch. I've memorized it and every detail and
even the curve of the sky above and it's strangely cold in Texas
this time of year and things are just getting colder and colder
and yesterday morning there was frost on the ground and I said
"What will this bring?" like that had an answer or someone to
answer it.

Carry me through this,
I beg you, carry me through this,
Make light this load as I bear it
There's a... Please carry me
Through this.

Each daughter blossomed in her own way and, of course, my
son My Son my son he is My Son, but each one of them
blossomed in their own way and I know that this divorce is
going to TRAMPLE ON THE FOREST FLOOR and each one of their
blossoms like the needles in the brush will be broken, but
maybe they will know that I am thinking, yes, I am thinking even
now and can a note here or there be the tendon tying to a
father's love? For what of his love, he who is gone? He sent no
notes, but I felt his love. I felt it like a piece of me and feel it still,
even though he is gone (not yet in the ground). I feel it still and

can only think each of them will feel me the same, in them, and not poisoned yet by the cankerous disease finally to be severed and I don't know, but I can only think that they will be okay.

In a rotted tree,
if you scrape away
the bark,
you can still find
a healthy root
that's untouched
by decay.

The time will come to make arrangements. Everyone will look to me to lead them. I am the hand to move this forward now. My hands are the hands. They will look to me. All these suits I must still wear. All this bark I must scrape away. They will look to me to be untouched, to amputate, to shake and guide and moan and stand firmly, like a man, over a box as it's put into the ground. Can I even mourn a man who knew love like that? Can I even mourn a man? Can I even mourn?

He lived to be ninety-two.

But he's gone. Evelyn's gone too. She's been gone for some time, but now it's official and there will be much paperwork and much discussion and third parties and pens and signatures and seals and copies and things in triplicate, like the tendril of the city creeping in through a back door left carelessly open and waiting to poison this well the same as ever, and even when you thought you'd weaned yourself from its bitter fruit, you find yourself back and suckling and gripping your hands and pressing out your pants. And the children will all say "divorce," and the blossoms, the needles, will all be under the hooves like those I remember back from the plank.

In a fluttering voice,
"My parents are divorced."
"My grandfather died."
These are things that will be said. And nothing but the abashed look away to the ground, to the dirt, to find the blood which seeks me out, ever and after, to cry aloud for all the things that won't ever be.

Children are like the needles in the forest and on the forest floor they lay and beasts come and beasts go, trampling, trampling, trampling. One is a ladybug and another one is a squirrel and the other one is a caterpillar and they are all needles, broken needles at that, and when Evelyn wanted to split last year, she got a place and moved away and thought that time apart would heal it all, but all the needles are always trampled and you can't fence in a beast that wants to run any more than the needles on the forest floor can withstand the rough, sooty hooves of rampaging creatures and there was a frost in this freak weather, before I even knew yesterday that one more thing had slid away from my center. You can already hear the hoofbeats of all that's on the horizon coming closer and closer. You can hear it. You can.

What has happened to my family?
Has my father set his house in order?
Have I? Can I?
I heard the rustle of the deer in the brush long before I saw him.

Swore I'd never wear a suit again. I shuffled off that coil a ways back and didn't ever plan on its return. But here I am and there are numbers to be discussed and now, with all this, with all this feeling, we'll push it all down, me and Evelyn and the girls and my son and pretend to deal strictly in business and say that we are sad and speak our emotions through a filter of untruth while the numbers are cold on the paper in front of us and yes, father, you did very well in your life. You did very well. And we'll now squabble for the prizes and it is worthwhile, but still, and you want your children to have a bright future and a life without pain and worry and to do all the things they dream to do, but still, but still why is it purchased with the blood like the meat on the deer that I saw him skin when I missed with the kill shot and then gave unto it mercy and God's bountiful bounty and the steaks in the freezer and all of our sustenance is built from the blood of that which has fallen by our hands and taken our pain and forgiven our cruelty and will my family live with the guilt of the blood or are they so different, or maybe not, as I wear this suit, are they so different to not care that the blood has spilled in the forest and cries out while the numbers add up and speak to them of their dreams? And father, I've done pretty well for myself you know. I've done pretty well for myself.

But I remember how he cut the hooves off.
For years afterwards I saw
the hooves being cut off
and sitting up on the plank
in the garage.
The hooves. Cut off.

But my mind hasn't slipped and I can still read the Bible and my memories are intact of years ago with the children and Evelyn and Sunday morning sweet potato pancakes, sweet and syrupy and us all sitting around the table together, when the children were children and the marriage was a marriage and my father was here and my wife was here and my children were here and now here is there and the table is empty and it's those moments after you hear it, thinking about how you'll never see him again, never in a hospital for him again, never again, that you think about how you woke up alone, sixty some years old, and how the white hair on your knuckles shook from the heater that blew on you as you read the Bible to yourself and sent out letters to those you still love, even if they don't love you, or don't remember you, but maybe they do and are too caught up in the numbers and the tendrils, but deep down they love as they have always loved and

When you saw
the deer on the ground,
its neck rolled back and forth,
its eye spun around in its head.
PUT IT DOWN.
The blood from the wound trickled into the ground,
his voice from above you saying PUT IT DOWN.
It doesn't even look at you as you steady your aim.
The needles on the floor are crushed underfoot.
It's mercy, you say, it's mercy.
It's mercy, he says. It's mercy.
It's mercy, he says, go on and put it out of its pain, he says.
Your finger is hot and cold and you tremble.

DYSTROPIA

I consider myself a normal person trying to live a normal life. I usually log out of virtuadream around 6:45 in the morning, when the automated light simulator panel switches from "night" to "day", reminding me that for only 6000ID per year I can license the "dawn" transition, a perennial bestseller in diurnal replication. I can't remember the last time I had that much money, but if I had it now, I sure wouldn't waste it on "dawn".

There's always that moment when I first wake up that I forget my left arm is disabled. Like most folks, I lost it in the war, which is no big deal, since veterans are entitled to free prosthesis for any loss of limb considered necessary for duty, which an arm surely is in most cases, but as the years have gone on and my stipend from the service has been reduced every year to help support the ongoing war effort, I haven't been able to afford the software licenses Prosthetitech requires, so they disabled my arm remotely, assuring me that they would turn it back on as soon as I relicense it at current rates and pay a small reactivation fee. I don't regret the war though. If we hadn't done what we did, we would never have secured the natural resources necessary for the increasing demand of our prostheses industry.

I don't spend too long looking at myself in the mirror. It's an old mirror, so the camera's not very good and the image glitches and lags when I move. I haven't upgraded it to Pro yet, so I still get ads, which can be annoying when I'm trying to brush my teeth and a window opens over my face to tell me that "brushing is a thing of the past with HappyMouth synthetic teeth". No shit, everyone knows that. So I swipe my thumb across the biometric scanner on the toilet and the lid opens automatically, assuring me that I am licensed to dispose of personal waste in this receptacle.

My wife boots up around 7:30. She's a 4-series, so her vocal and facial expressions are fairly limited and her maintenance costs are high, but I love her. She interfaces with the sustenance dispenser and fills a small glass full of Monsanto xanthan gum nutrient paste and brings it to me. I swallow breakfast in a couple gulps. Couldn't tell you how it tastes, since my senses of smell and taste were irreparably damaged by prolonged exposure to toxic chemicals during my stint as a sub-crust miner, but it gets the job done, eliminating hunger for two to three hours.

My wife reminds me that the sustenance dispenser hardware is no longer supported and that I will need to replace it if I want to receive the latest Xanthan formula. She recommends the Foodblaster Plus, now only 8600ID. I don't know why we'd want some fancy thing like that, but she can't help herself. Her recommendation algorithm is hardwired into her empathy circuit and she's only trying to bring me products that would improve my life.

We sit together in front of the wall screen during the mandatory entertainment hour, as my biodata and her utility metrics are synched with the main servers. As usual, the health counselor app informs me of my disabled arm and a whole slew of other problems, the cures for which far exceed my bronze-tier health allotment. I leave the apartment around 9 for work. My wife shuts down for the day, she's only licensed between 7:30-9AM and 5:30-9PM, which works great for my schedule.

Outside of the apartment, I activate my neural HUD, the unfortunate consequence of which is my ID balance staring me in the face. I wasn't selected to be rich during the last class lottery, but I'm grade 76, which means there are at least 24 grades of people worse off than me. Don't know how they manage to get by, but ever since they outlawed intergrade mingling, it hasn't been much of a problem. The GPS highlights the yellow route to work, even though I've walked it every day for years. If I decide to go a different way, the deviation is recorded and sent back to the health counselor for analysis.

All you see on the street these days are these damn SOLIPspheres. They came out a year ago or so and now everyone uses them. Cream colored spheres for citizens grade 21-100 (though I doubt anyone above a grade 50 could afford one), black spheres for grades 1-20, blue spheres for police and so on. "Secure. Opaque. Luxurious. Immaculate. Private." I see the commercials all the time. Basically, it's a hovering ball that you sit in and it has screens and all kinds of things inside it. They've become more and more common and I see fewer faces each time I walk to work, which is fine by me, since most of the time I'm focused on my HUD.

Cops tend to not trust people outside of SOLIPspheres, so occasionally I get harangued by some blue balls. Again, it's not that big of a deal. I just lie face down on the ground while they scan my biodata and read my history. It's not like I have any weapons or books or other contraband, so I have nothing to worry about. They always let me go with a warning and a reminder that if I purchase the Good Citizen module I can reduce random police stops by 30%. But I'm awfully glad to have the police around, even if it means gravel on my face, because occasionally I'll see them stopping someone who has some sort of illegal possession or body mod and then they really go to work. They're also the only ones keeping the Grade 100s in the tunnels.

Like most people, I code for a living. I'm constantly writing, re-writing, updating and deleting code for thousands of applications across the world. Even a grade 100 can eat every day if they buckle down in their tunnel compartment and code for ten hours. None of us design whole systems, of course, the work is parceled out in such a way that we don't really know what we're working on, just how to create or repair sections of code that are assigned to us. "Coding makes the world" is a popular saying. I could code faster if I had use of my other arm, which would result in increased pay, but even as I am, I keep my apartment licensed and my sustenance dispenser refilled.

About once a week or so, the whole cube farm is evacuated into the underground freedom bunkers because of another terrorist threat. Usually it's New Philisita, barbaric technophobes who hate us for our innovation and success, but sometimes it's the right wing militias who want to further segregate the grades, or sometimes it's nothing at all, just a drill to keep us sharp. I don't follow politics much, it's below my pay grade, as I like to say to my wife. It always makes her laugh. Anyway, after the police clear the building and scan all us employees, it's back to business as usual. "Code won't write itself!" is another popular motto, although somewhat deprecated, since programs have been writing code for almost ten years now, and could possibly eliminate the need for human coders within the next five years.

Cubicle walls are sound proofed, but each cubicle comes with a personal valet app that will answer questions and even engage in brief conversations during sanctioned break periods. I've been through three generations of the cubicle valet and I am still amazed at what technology can do. It's almost like having another person right here in my private work cube.

If I have any errands, I run them after work. I have a 30 minute lunch break, but we haven't been able to leave the premises since New Philistia bombed a coding center a few years back. The increased security is a little inconvenient, but I'd much rather drink lunch in my cube than get blown up by a bloodthirsty maniac. The state offices are downtown and since it's too far to walk, especially with the militarized prosperity checkpoints, I usually take the Skytram.

The only people on the tram these days are high-graders, any of whom could be strapped with explosives or hopped up on drugs. I try to mind my own business, letting the admittedly out-of-date security protocol of my HUD assess threats nearby. I've never been hacked myself, but they say people without the latest firmware are vulnerable to all kinds of exploits. I heard a story a while back about a terrorist who wasn't even a terrorist at all, just some shmuck whose neural interface got manipulated. He blew himself and thirty other people up in a state office waiting room. "Safety is a priority." That's what the commercials say for neural firmware. "A wise person will always upgrade themselves first."

The state offices, great skyscrapers huddled together, tower over the central district. Here, a blue SOLIPsphere patrols every corner and undercover police pose as high-graders, trying to get information about possible threats. The reason I'm here today is that I'm hoping to have a modification made to my health consultant app.

The reception terminal scans my biodata and gives me number 4F23A, ordering me to sit in the waiting area. There aren't any available chairs, so I stand with the others in a corner of the waiting area, coding on my projection keyboard some projects I wasn't able to finish up at work. The light simulator panels in state offices are always set to "day". Since state offices achieved full automation, they've been open 24/7. By the time my number is called, a couple of hours have passed. It doesn't bother me that much, since I would have just coded at home, although I do miss seeing my wife in the evening. Hopefully I'll get home before 9.

I'm brought into an "assistance and consultation room," which consists of a chair and a wall screen. After I sit down and am scanned again, the advertisements begin, with a notice that my consultation will begin in five minutes. I sit through the ads, maintaining the required amount of eye contact with the screen, and finally am greeted by a CGI image of a woman in office attire who asks me what she can do for me today.

I explain that every morning, when my biodata is synched with the servers, I get a notice that my prosthesis is unlicensed. I can't afford to license it, at least not at the rate I can code with only one arm, so it doesn't look like I'll be fixing it in the near future. All I want is for the notifications to be turned off, so that I can go through my day without being reminded that my arm doesn't work, something that happens anyway, whenever I try to use it.

First, she suggests that I license the arm, offering a plethora of informational videos about the benefits of fully licensed prostheses. I explain again that I can't afford it. She calculates my grade and coding ability (based on the data constantly being collected on me) and informs me that I should be able to afford the license. I tell her that those numbers are based on the coding ability of two hands, and that with only one hand, I code much slower, thus reducing my productivity. A reduction in productivity is not desirable, she informs me. I ask again for the notifications to be turned off. She asks me if I'm unhappy and then, before I answer, diagnoses me with General Dissatisfaction. The screen turns off and a receipt is printed out, ordering me to proceed to floor 4 for treatment. I can't argue with her (the wall screen is off), so I leave the room and am guided to the fourth floor by various disembodied voices and light patterns.

On the fourth floor, an automated walkway shuffles me between various scanners. A wall screen at the end of the walkway reiterates that I suffer from General Dissatisfaction and asks me to place my head in a metallic harness. I put the harness on with some difficulty and almost immediately two sets of prongs pry open my eyelids so I can't close them. A laser shoots into my left eyeball.

Back on the Skytram and I'm feeling great. I have to hand it to the state offices, they really know their stuff. It didn't even bother me when the Skytram was stopped for 20 minutes while police ushered a grade 90 into an isolation pod. I hurry back to my apartment through nearly empty streets to get in before the temporary curfew kicks in.

Unfortunately, 9 o'clock has come and gone and my wife has entered hibernation for the night. I walk over to her and pat her on the hair-like polymer with my good arm. Her face panel animates briefly as she asks if I would like to license "late night intimacy" tonight. I check my HUD, even though I know I can't afford it, and decline. Her face panel resumes its expressionless inertia and she says nothing else.

I spend my last minutes awake regretting that my DNA wasn't chosen for replication by the state procreation board. Even though I would probably never get to actually meet my offspring, it would've been nice knowing that I had contributed to the propagation of the human race. But, I'm lucky enough to have a significant other, and even though she's a few series behind and sits inert in a corner, silently collecting data on me, I don't feel quite so alone.

So here I sit, in my artificially lit apartment, with an offline wife, a jar full of room temperature xanthan gum, a disabled arm, hardly an international dollar to my name, a coding job that doesn't earn me enough money to license the prosthesis I got in the war, and a newly administered cure for my General Dissatisfaction that made it impossible for me to express discontent in any way. But I can't complain.

NOLI ME TANGERE

He is in a room.

The room is not large. The room is not small. There is a metal table in the middle of the room. There is a body on the table. He stands over the body. On one wall is a large mirror. He is told it is a one-way mirror. He is told the analyst watches from behind the mirror. He is told not to worry about the analyst, to continue on as he normally would. On the opposite wall is the door. The door is closed. The door is locked. Next to the table is a large metal tray on a stand. The tray holds many implements. There are mirrors. There are scalpels. There are others. Also in the room is the woman. She stands next to the tray. She wears a green mask over her nose and mouth. He cannot see her nose and mouth. She wears a cover over her hair and body. He cannot see her hair or body. Her eyes stand out from the suit. He can see her eyes. She looks at him expectantly.

He wears a similar outfit to hers. His outfit is green. His hands are covered in green gloves. He is very clean. The room is very clean. The table is very clean. The mirror is very clean. The woman is very clean. He is told everything must be very clean in order to proceed. He is told the implements must be sterile before they can be used. He is told sterility is important. He is told cleanliness is important.

He looks from the woman to the mirror. He looks from the mirror to the table. There is a body on the table. The body appears to be that of a man. The man is older and has gray hair. The man is in decent shape, though has a bit of a gut. He is naked on the table. The man's penis is flaccid. The man's tongue protrudes slightly from his mouth. The man's skin is pale and blue around the edges. The man's veins show up against his skin. The man has no expression. The man's eyes are closed. He cannot see the man's eyes.

He looks from the body on the table back to the woman. The woman looks at him expectantly. He looks at the mirror. He sees himself in the mirror. He is told the analyst watches through the mirror. He does not see the analyst. He looks at himself in the mirror expectantly. He takes no action.

The woman shifts slightly to the left. She brings her left hand up towards her face and tightens her glove. She lowers her hand. She does not look at the body on the table. She does not look at the mirror. She does not look at the door. She looks alternately between him and herself. He rolls his eyes and scans the room again. There is the mirror, the table with the body, the door, the woman. He rolls his eyes again.

"Uh...what are we..." he says.
"Doctor, if you please," she says. She makes no motions.
"Doctor...right...uh...what is this...patient's...condition?" he asks her.
"The patient awaits surgery."
"...Isn't the patient dead?"
"Yes, doctor."
"Quite."

He examines the tray next to the table. He examines the implements. His eyes linger on each tool, one by one, down the line. He looks from the tray to the mirror. He sees himself in the mirror. He looks to the woman. She looks at him expectantly.

"Right," he says. "Uh,"
"Yes, doctor?" she says.
"...Scalpel...?"

She reaches down, grabs the first scalpel and hands it to him handle first. He hesitates. He looks at the mirror. He cannot see the analyst. He looks at the woman. She looks at him expectantly. He looks at the body. He cannot see the man's eyes. He takes the scalpel.

He holds the scalpel in his right hand. "Right," he says. "Uh..." He places his left hand on the body's stomach. He looks at his hand. He looks at the mirror. He looks at the woman.

"Well then," he says. He moves his hand slowly around the body's torso. He watches the woman while he does this. Her expression does not change. She looks at him expectantly.

"Right," he says.

He lowers the scalpel to the body's flesh. He checks the mirror again. He sees himself, holding the scalpel to the body's flesh. He looks at her again. She looks at him expectantly. He looks back to his hand. He places the scalpel slightly below and to the right of the navel. He gently presses the blade of the scalpel into the flesh of the body. Blood immediately begins to seep out from the cut, down the side of the flesh and onto the metal table. The blood begins to pool on the table. The blood pools on the metal table.

"Uh...can you...do something... about the uh, blood?" he says.
"Yes, doctor," she says. She pulls a suction device out from
beneath the tray and begins sucking the blood off of the table.
Soon all the blood is gone and she holds it against the incision.

He looks at the mirror. He sees nothing. He can see nothing. He
listens closely. He has made the first incision.

YOU MUST INCISE

He hears it, he thinks. It may have come from behind the mirror.
Is it the voice of the analyst, he wonders. Perhaps, he answers.
It is not the woman's voice. The body is dead and cannot speak.
It may be his own voice, he cannot be sure. He must incise.

He drags the scalpel down the abdomen and into the pubis. She
sucks the blood. He has completed the first cut. He looks at the
cut, the mirror, the woman, the body, the tray.

"...clamp?" he says.
"Yes, doctor," she says. She hands him the first clamp.

He slowly peels the skin back where he has cut it. He peels back
the flap of skin. He peels it back and can see beneath it the
organs. He uses the clamp to hold the flap open.

"The blood?" he says.
"Yes, doctor," she says. She sucks the blood out.

He can see the organs now. He can see inside. The organs are
wound inside tightly. The organs fit perfectly. Inside the torso

cavity, the organs fit snugly against one another. There is much blood. She sucks the blood out.

YOU MUST REMOVE THE ORGANS

"Uh..." he says.
"Yes, doctor?" she says.
"I must remove the organs."
"Yes, doctor." She makes no motion.
"Right."

He reaches down into the torso and feels the first organ. It is the intestine. He feels the intestine through his glove. He can feel its texture. He can feel its weight. He holds the intestine and looks at the mirror. He sees himself holding the intestine. He cannot see the analyst. He looks at her. She looks at him expectantly. He looks at the body. The eyes are closed. The intestine is in his hand. He pulls.

YOU MUST REMOVE THE ORGANS

He pulls and pulls and pulls and pulls.

"Something to uh put this in?" he says.
"Yes, doctor," she says. She retrieves a large metal bucket out from under the table. He places the intestines in the bucket. He continues removing the organs. He places the organs inside the bucket.

"What...what exactly...what exactly are we doing here?" he says.
"Doctor?" she says.

"What exactly are we doing here? Are you going to uh measure these organs?"

"No, doctor."

"Right…Then, uh, why are we uh…are you taking notes on what we are doing?"

"No, doctor."

"The analyst must be taking notes."

"The analyst, doctor?"

"Uh…yeah…he's uh, behind that mirror, right?"

"Doctor, that is just a mirror. Behind the mirror is just a wall."

He stops removing the organs. He looks at his hands. They are covered in blood. He looks at the body. It is covered in blood. He looks at the table. It is covered in blood. He looks at the mirror. He sees himself (covered in blood). He looks at her. She looks at him expectantly.

"Then why…" he says.

YOU MUST REMOVE THE ORGANS
YOU MUST INCISE
YOU MUST REMOVE THE ORGANS

"Uh…" he says.

YOU MUST INCISE
"uh…"
YOU MUST INCISE
"uh…"

The door opens. An old man walks in. It is not the same old man on the table. He does not think it is the same old man that is on the table.

"What, uh, who are you?" he says.
"Young man. Young man. You know who I am," the old man says.
"No...No, I don't think we've met."

The old man laughs. The woman does not take notice of the old man. The woman looks at him expectantly. The woman remains silent.

"You must incise, dear boy. You must. You must remove the insides. You must cut and clean and remove the organs. These are things that you must do. These are things that must happen, do you understand? Dear boy, dear, dear boy. You must cut into the flesh. You must roll back the flesh. You must clamp the flesh. You must incise. You must remove the organs. You must you must you must," the old man says.

"Uh..." he says. "What?"

The woman looks at him. Her eyes are crazy and wild. She is unfocused. He looks at her. She opens her mouth.

"OH, I just got the LOVELIEST floor plant for my apartment. It is just DARLING. I got it on SPECIAL last weekend when I was out with the HUBBY. It is green and has BEAUTIFUL red flowers that are ALWAYS in bloom. We also got a NEW blender. It blends so NICELY. I saw it advertised on the TEEVEE. Hubby and I are SO HAPPY. We are really HOPING to have children SOON. We are really hoping. We really are. We really are," she says.

He looks at her. He looks to the body. He looks to the old man.

"The heart has many valves. The valves push and generate pressure. The valves must pump. The pressure must be maintained. The valves cannot be incised. The heart cannot be removed. It is connected to the vascular network. It must be connected to the vascular network. The heart must pump blood (with the valves) through the vascular network in order to serve the rest of the body, do you understand, dear boy?" the old man says.

"No...uh, not really," he says. "Can you get out of here? We're doing an operation or something, I think."

The old man immediately turns and leaves. The old man closes the door. He looks back to the woman.

"No one behind the mirror, huh?" he says.
"No, doctor," she says.
"Then who the hell was that? And what was all that stuff about a floor plant?"
"A floor plant, doctor? I don't know what you mean."
"Right."

He looks back to the body. There is no cut in the flesh. There is no blood. There is no clamp. The tools are lined perfectly along the tray. The man is warm and pink. The man is breathing. The man's eyes are closed. He cannot see the man's eyes.

"This man is alive!"
"Yes, doctor."
"Then the operation was a success!"

"You have not operated yet, doctor."

"Quite...uh..."

He looks to the mirror. He can almost make out a blinking red light behind the mirror. But he sees himself. He sees the woman. He sees the table. He sees the body. He sees the tray. In the mirror he sees these things. He can almost make out a blinking red light.

"Uh,"

"Yes, doctor?"

"What is the condition of the patient?"

"He is ready for surgery."

"Right."

Must he incise? Must he remove the organs? He looks at the woman. She looks at him expectantly. He looks at the mirror. He sees the things, almost makes out a blinking red light. He looks at the body on the table. He looks at the tray. He looks at the tools on the tray.

Must he incise?

Must he remove the organs?

There is no answer.

"Uh...scalpel?"

"Yes, doctor." She hands him the first scalpel on the table.

"Right."

He lowers the scalpel to the flesh. He touches the scalpel to the flesh.

Must he incise?
Must he remove the organs?
There is no answer.
He hesitates.

O EXPECTIMINIMAX TREE

1 - Jeffries, Jr. and Sr.

When the phone rang, Jeffrey Jr. took extra care to play quietly in his room so his father could hear the person who called. When Jeffrey made a lot of noise, his dad couldn't hear and sometimes phone calls were from very important people about very important things. Jeffrey did not think his stupid toys were more important than his father's phone calls. He would not make a racket again. He understood.

"Hello?...Oh...What is it?...When?"

Jeffrey Jr. held his toys softly, a car that turned into a T-Rex in one hand and a yellow crane operated by a smiling, hard-hatted man in the other, racing them just above the ground so they wouldn't make noise scraping the carpet. He looked at the pupilless eyes of the Dino-car and made it move back and forth over the ground, imagining it rumbling, roaring and speeding through his room. The man in the crane looked like a nice man. He wore a blue long-sleeved shirt, buttoned up the front, and blue jeans. His little cuffed hands gripped the levers of the crane, which, although Jeffrey Jr. couldn't detach the hands from the levers, or even move the levers, cause of how it was built, being plastic and all, he imagined they swiveled the crane left and right, raised the arm up and down, dropped and retrieved the hook.

"Well-...I know it's important."

He placed the crane on the ground in front of him. He imagined the crane operator going to work every day with his hard hat and his metal lunchbox, to a skyscraper construction site, where, from the ground, the buildings rose up into the air so the tops couldn't even be seen through the clouds.

"Fine...No, it's fine...Thirty minutes...Yeah...Yeah."

Jeffrey Jr. jolted as his dad tossed the cordless phone onto the counter.

"Kath!"
"...What?"
"You need to watch him for a while. I have to go into work."
"You what?"
"I'm going into to work."
"When?"
"Right now. I'm going in right now. Jesus Christ."

His dad rustled through the hall closet and coats sagged to the floor as they fell from their hangers. His dad yanked out his brown work jacket. Jeffrey turned the crane slowly. The crane operator grabbed a giant iron girder from the ground and lifted it mightily into place. Jeffrey's dad now picked through the fallen coats, cursing, trying to find his brown shoes. He pulled out the first brown shoe and tossed it behind him. He dug some more, pulled out a black shoe, threw the black shoe back into the closet, dug some more, pulled out the other brown shoe, stood, and slammed the closet shut. Jeffrey made his other toy, now in car form, drive around the crane, still well above the floor, as even though the phone had been hung up, he knew well enough that his dad worked very hard for him and his mother and that nobody appreciated his dad and that everyone should stay out of his way when he had work to do so he could put food in their mouths.

His dad left through the front door, slamming it behind him, and Jeffrey Jr. waited ten seconds after he heard his dad's truck roll over their gravel driveway before moving. He stood up, taking his toys with him. He entered his parents' bedroom where his mom lay sleeping on the bed.

"Mom?"
"What is it?"
"What are you doing?"
"I'm trying to sleep."
"Mom?"
"What?"
"Can I play in here?"
"Can you play quiet? I need to get some sleep."
"All right."
"...Play for a little minute, then go play outside. *We* played outside as kids, you know."
"All right, mom."

Jeffrey Jr. sat cross-legged between his dad's sweatshirt and a taped up cardboard box in the corner of the room by the hamper and set his toys down. The plastic clicked as he turned the pieces of the Dino-car so it vaguely resembled a T-Rex. He put the T-Rex down by the crane.

Look out, crane guy, it's a monster! Ahhhh! But the crane operator would swing the crane around and hit the T-Rex in the head with a girder. The T-Rex might try to bite the crane operator, but he was safe inside the steel cab and the T-Rex's teeth would all break and fall out if he tried to bite him. The T-Rex didn't stand a chance.

2 - William and Jeffrey, Jrs.

"Dude, that crane sucks," William Jr. said.

"It's all right. I like it," Jeffrey Jr. replied.

"Not as much as Dino-car."

"No, not as much. Dino-car is awesome!"

"Yeah, the Dino-car is the best. Let me be him this time, if you're so big on the crane."

"I wanna be him this time. I just got him and he's mine so I should get him first."

"Yeah, cause I gave him to you. Since I gave him to you, you should let me play with him whenever I want. You can take him home and stuff, but when we play, I get to be him if I want."

"That's no fair! You said I could have him and so I should get to be him."

"What am I supposed to be, the crane?"

"Why not?"

"Because, the crane sucks. I don't even own one of those. I don't want to be some stupid guy in a crane, especially against the Dino-car."

"The guy in the crane could take the Dino-car..."

"Hahaha like how? T-Rex is the best dinosaur. A guy wouldn't stand a chance. T-Rex would rip that guy in half."

"Not in the crane."

"Yes in the crane. T-Rex would rip the crane open like a tin can and gobble him up like in Jurassic Park."

"No, the T-Rex would try to open the crane and break all his teeth on the steel. Then the guy would hit the T-Rex in the head with a giant metal beam."

"No."

"Yeah, he would."

"I'm gonna be the T-Rex and the T-Rex wins against a crane."

"Not against a spaceship."

"You don't have a spaceship."

"It could be."

"No, it's a crane. It can't change into a spaceship unless it really changes into a spaceship. That's why Dino-car is so cool, dumbass."

"If I'm going to be the crane, then the crane has to be able to win too."

"Not against the Dino-car."

"Then I don't want to play."

"Fine, then I don't either."

"Then I'm going home."

"Well, gimme back the Dino-car then."

"What? No way, you gave him to me."

"I want it back. You're so into crane guy anyway."

"You can't take it back now, Indian giver, he's mine and you said I could take him home."

"I changed my mind! Give him back!!"

"No way!"

"I'll tell."

"So?"

"So, I'll tell my dad."

"So?"

"So, my dad is the boss of your dad and your dad will be in trouble."

"Nuh uh."

"Yeah, I heard my dad say that he's your dad's boss."

"So?"

"So? So that pretty much makes me the boss of you."

"No it doesn't."

"Are you going to give him back?"

"Come on, you gave him to me."

"Are you?"

"Will..."

"Are you?"

"You gave him to me..."

"I only gave him to you because your Christmas presents always suck and I knew you'd cry if you didn't get something cool."

"My presents don't suck."

"Remember when you told me how much cooler my family was then yours when you came over yesterday?"

"Yeah, but,"

"And how much better my house is?"

"Yeah, but,"

"And how you wished we were brothers?"

"That's not what-"

"Just give me back the Dino-car, Jeff. You got to play with him some, didn't you?"

"I'm not giving him back!"

"Fine, then I'll take him back."

"Let go!"

"Got him!"

"Give me back the crane!"

"It's my crane now. I'll trade you for Dino-car."

"Give me back the crane! It's not yours!"

"Get off me! Let go!"

"Give it!"

"I don't want this stupid thing anyway!"

"You broke it!"

"No, you broke it! Give me back the Dino-car!"

"No way!"

"Fine, but I'm telling!"

"Go ahead! My dad will beat your dad up and you!!"

"In your dreams!"

3 - Williams, Sr. and Jr.

The smell of fresh blueberry scones wafted over William Sr. as he opened the front door of his house, the wreath tapping as it jostled, and stepped inside. His wife stood in the kitchen at the mixer, smiling at its consistent hum, her eyes lost in the revolutions of its blades. She yelled hello from where she stood and William greeted her happily. He removed his boots by the door, carefully brushing off the snow. He hung his new pea coat, a Christmas gift from his wife, on the woodgrain wall-hanger and crossed the tile floor in his socks. He embraced his wife and kissed her on the neck, telling her that the scones smelled delicious. She told him how she had bagged blueberries from the farmer's market and kept them in the garage freezer so she could bake with them in the winter. He appreciated her forethought and greatly anticipated reaping its rewards.

Finally! What he had been waiting for all day: his leather recliner. The gas fireplace already burned safely behind its glass, where Christmas cards of friends and neighbors perched above on the tinseled mantle. His wife brought him some coffee and told him it would be about twenty-five minutes for the scones. He nuzzled into the plush chair and looked at his Christmas tree, now without presents it was just the golden skirt hiding the metal stand of the synthetic tree. But it made him happy. It reminded him of yesterday morning. Just how lucky he and his family were! He always tried to feel the proper amount of awe and gratitude for the blessings he had received.

He asked his wife if William Jr. was home. She told him that Will had come home a few hours ago, but had been in his room. He had looked upset when he came home. Out with Jeffrey, she said. He looked at his wife with dissatisfaction. His son maintained an intermittent friendship with Jeffrey's son and the last time they got into a fight, William Sr. had thought of forbidding their interaction. He relented, of course, to the pleas of his son and allowed them to be friends again with the strict understanding that they were not to quarrel – or at least to settle it themselves. He assumed from the expression on his wife's face that they hadn't, and that it would be up to him to deal with it. He was used to it, being where the buck stopped, and, to be perfectly honest with himself, he relished the role.

He knocked on his son's door. The timbre of his son's voice as he said 'come in' through the door clued him in to the severity of the fight. He stepped inside. The TV flashed with a Christmas movie next to an open box of peppermint sticks. Comics and toys were scattered on the floor. Will really needed to clean his room. His son lay on his bed, reading one of the new comic books he had gotten yesterday.

"You doing all right, buddy?"
"Yeah."
"Your mother said you were upset when you came home."
"...Yeah, I guess."
"Want to tell me about it?"

His son put down the comic book and paused for a moment, gathering his thoughts.

"Jeffrey Jr. stole my Dino-car! The one you gave me for Christmas."

"We didn't get you a... Oh, last Christmas. He stole it? That doesn't sound like Jeff."

"He has it right now!"

"And he stole it?"

"Well..."

"Accusing someone of stealing is a very serious thing, Will. If you're lying about it, tell me the truth right now and you won't be in trouble."

"Okay, well, he didn't steal it. I sort of... gave it to him yesterday."

"You gave it to him?"

"Yeah, I mean, I thought I wanted to, because of how he never gets anything good for Christmas. But then he wouldn't let me play with it today! And since I gave it to him, I should be able to play with it whenever I want, right?"

"You can't just give your toys away, Will."

"Well I tried to get it back! But he wouldn't give it back and he called me an Indian giver!"

"You shouldn't have given it to him in the first place. I work hard so I can afford to buy you the toys you get for Christmas, the house you live in, the food you eat. Did you think about that before you just gave it away?"

"...I guess not..."

"Well you should have. What if I just gave away what my father gave to me, or his father to him?"

"I don't know."

"We wouldn't have anything at all. Do you understand?"

"I guess so... Does this mean he gets to keep Dino-car?"

"...I'll go over to Jeffery's and have a talk with his father. I'm sure he'll understand the mix up and get your toy back. But I want to make sure this doesn't happen again, so I've got to punish you too."

"Daaad!"

"You made a mistake, buddy. It's not a terrible one, and this time it won't cost you anything real, but we need to make sure this is the last time you make it, okay?"

"... All right."

"I'm going to hang on to your toy for a week, so you can think about what it would have been like if you had lost it for good. If we can make it through the next week without any more incidents, especially anything involving Jeffrey Jr., you can have it back. Sound fair?"

"Sounds fair, dad."

"All right. Good talk."

He stood and his son turned his attention back to the comic book. William Sr. felt very lucky indeed to have as well-behaved a son as he did, considering how kids were these days. He could have a talk with his son and work things out, tell the truth, and still be his friend while punishing him when he got out of line. He decided to go share their talk with his wife and then head back out into the snow right away to see Jeffrey Sr. for the second time today.

4 - Jeffrey and William, Srs.

Women and kids don't know what it means to work. Even women who work, most of em, don't know, cause they got husbands who also work. And anyway, working for them is some kind of pride thing, to prove they're equal or something. No need to worry about that with Kath, of course. I'm lucky if the house is halfway clean half the time when I get home during the week. She can't even look after the kid, which is supposed to be a woman's bread and butter. She lets the guy wander outside doing who knows what and doesn't think it's strange that he keeps coming home in one piece. She doesn't know what it's like out there, is why.

My work is a tax on my life. It's a condition of living, a price I pay to savor the few spare minutes in between when someone isn't asking something of me or telling me what to do or upset because I'm doing something I actually enjoy. That's not to say I don't take pride in what I do. You better believe I do. I may not like it, and I might complain about it, but I do it well and I am proud that I provide for my family to the best of my ability, and sure, we don't have too much, not like a lot of people do, but we get by, which a lot of people can't.

I hadn't even sat down for five minutes or cracked the beer I pulled out of the freezer before someone started knocking at the door.

"Kath! Someone's at the door!"
"I can't get it right now!"

No, of course not, not even this. Nope, not even this. So I got myself up, out of my chair, and opened the door. Now I fully acknowledge that I have a temper and that in some situations I can overreact, but when I saw Bill standing in my doorway, I thought my head was going to explode. The nerve of this guy, to call me in to work in the morning is enough; I mean, I almost went postal once already today. Now he comes by my place? The fucking nerve.

"What is it, Bill?"

"Hi Jeffrey, how are you?"

"All right. What can I do for you?"

"There seems to have been an issue- "

"No way. I double checked it. Everything was right when I left earlier."

"...What I was going to say was that there seems to have been an issue with our boys."

"Our boys?"

"That's right. I'm awfully sorry to bother you here at home, but I thought it best to talk it over face to face."

"What's the problem?"

"Can I come in?"

"...All right."

So I let Bill in, but stood there, waiting for him to get to his point. I let him in, it's only common courtesy, even though I could gut the bastard, but still, I wasn't offering him a beer, I wasn't asking him to have a seat. God only knew what these little bastards got into and what Bill's expecting me to do, but I swore by Christ if he was here to bilk me out of more money, I would end his life. Jail or not, the chair or not, I'd choke him out, sit down and drink my beer.

"So, what's the problem?"

"Apparently, your son has one of Will's toys."

"You're saying he stole it?"

"No, no, no, not at all. Not at all."

"Well, what then?"

"In a... lapse of judgment, as kids often have, Will 'gave' one of his toys, one he's rather fond of, to Jeff for Christmas."

"And...?"

"And... He didn't have permission to give his toys away. He made a mistake and I'm here to get the toy back."

This guy called me in the day after Christmas, a holiday AND a weekend and he's concerned with some fucking toy? Was he pulling my leg?

"Uh..."

"Look, Jeffrey, you and I know how it is. If the roles were reversed, I know you'd be in the same position that I am and it would be you standing in my living room right now, asking me."

"..."

"Hopefully, I would understand that children don't quite grasp the concept of property, of impulse, of hard work and so forth."

"Is that so?"

"Jeffrey, I'm not looking to give you a hard time, to accuse anyone of anything, or to cause you or your son any trouble. In fact, it's my son who made a mistake, and I would like to apologize to you and to Jeff Jr. on his behalf."

"That's all right."

"No, I insist. It's important to teach these kids about right and wrong, about acting responsibly, as you well know. I'm only trying to do my part as a father to look out after my son, as you no doubt do for yours."

"All right. Let me get him. Jeffrey!"

"Thank you. Again, sorry for the trouble."

"Yeah, like I said it's no problem. JEFF!"

"Yes?"

"You got one of Will Jr.'s toys?"

"He gave it to me! For Christmas!"

"Go get it."

"But Dad, he…"

"Go get it now. Bill, I'd like to get this cleared up right away. I have some things to take care of tonight, so if you don't mind, I'll get you the toy and back about your business."

"It's no problem."

"Is that it?"

"Yeah, but…"

"Hand it over."

"But dad…"

"Now!"

"But dad, Will broke my crane, the one I got for Christmas!"

"Will didn't say anything to me about that, Jeff. Are you sure?"

"Yes, sir! He broke it, trying to get back the Dino-car!"

"I don't know anything about that, Jeffrey."

"Yeah, me either. Anyway, give him back Will's toy."

"…All right."

"Thank you. All right, Bill. Sorry for the trouble."

"If you don't mind, can I speak to young Jeff for a moment?"

"That's not necessary, really."

"I insist. Please, I told my son I would."

"I guess it's all right."

"Jeff, thank you for giving Will back his toy. I want to apologize to you from him, because I know you thought the toy was yours. I'm punishing him for lying to you about it, because he was the one in the wrong here. Anyway, when you grow up and have your own kids, you'll understand better."

"Yes, sir."

"All right, Bill. I really need to get back to it."

"Of course. Thanks for your time. See you on Monday."

I closed the door behind him, barely able to see straight. Brass fucking balls. Comes into MY house, tells MY kid what's what? Sure I wanted to break his face. What am I gonna do? Beat him up? Which I could, easily. So easily. Maybe if we lived in the wild west when men could settle things between each other. But today, I'd just get thrown in jail, my family would starve, and he'd be back at work on Monday, wearing his bruises like a badge of courage! Fuck him and fuck this world. I'd have to take it nice and slow, wait until there wasn't anything between us, until long after I quit, which I will someday, and won't he be fucked then, but after I quit, some night, years later maybe, show up and just beat him to death on his driveway. I need that beer.

See, though, kids and women. Can't even keep a brand new toy for one fucking day. It's already broke.

"Jeff!"
"Yeah, dad?"
"How did the crane get broken?"
"Will broke it!"
"I don't care who broke it! I just got that for you. Maybe if you cared more about the toys you already have, instead of the ones your little friends have, you'd still have an unbroken crane."
"Yes, sir."

Kids these days are spoiled to death. Think things just fall from the sky. Think they deserve something just cause it exists. Without working for it. Sweating for it. Day in and day out. Bill lecturing me about raising kids. He's right, though, even if it isn't his place to say. Well, by God, my son's not growing up that way. He's going to learn the value of a hard day's work if it kills me

SINE WAVE

There's sand. Maybe it's sawdust.

He moves it from one pile to another in his hotel room.

"What are you doing?" she says.

"It came out of the wall," he says.

He moves it from one pile to another. They are in the Hotel Pickwick.

"I want to go shopping," she says.

"Well, go," he says.

She picks at her lips. She has lipstick on her finger.

He is moving the sand. Or sawdust.

"Let's go," she says.

"Hold on." He is digging now, into the pile. There's a root.

"Where did that come from?" she says.

"How should I know?" he says.

"I don't know."

"Me either."

"Well, let's go out."

"Fine."

He stands up and has sawdust or sand on his knees. She doesn't say anything.

He puts on his sport coat and opens the hotel room door.

The lock clicks out of place.

He briefly sees past the closing door of the room across the hall. A thin, elegant blonde with the reddest lipstick he's ever seen is tongue kissing a brunette with pale skin in a black evening dress.

The door closes.

She follows him into the hall.

"What were you looking at?" she says.

"Nothing." he says.

*

"The Pickwick's right on Union Square," she says.

"No, the Francis Drake is on Union Square. This is *near* Union Square," he says.

There is traffic on the streets.

There is garbage on the streets.

They walk across Market to the other sidewalk, past the steel rolling gate of a camera shop.

"It's not open yet," he says.

She says nothing. Her heels clack on the ground. He looks at her hair in the streetlight.

It's not as blonde as when they first met.

"What do you want for dinner?" she says.

"I don't care," he says.

"You always make me do this. Why do I always have to pick?"

"All right then, Italian."

She keeps walking.

Homeless people sleep in doorways, in the alleys between buildings.

"What were you doing in the room?" she says.

"I was moving it," he says.

"Moving what?"

"It was sand. Maybe sawdust. From the walls."

"Maybe it's from the construction. The Pickwick is under construction."

"Maybe."

It is cold outside. They reach union square. Many people mill about.

"Not here," he says.

They continue walking down Market.

*

"We're going to be at the wharf if you keep this up," she says.

"We're almost there," he says.

"My feet hurt."

Piping and cabling run up and down the brick walls.

Stores on the bottom floor. Apartments on the upper floors.

Light from a window.

A middle aged man in a sleeveless shirt sits in a worn recliner.

He watches television.

He shines in the light of the television.

"What are you looking at?" she says.

"Nothing," he says.

They stop at an alley. A sign. It says something.

"Cafe Tiramisu," she says.

"Yeah," he says.

"Sounds good."

"Yeah."

She examines the menu behind the glass casing attached to the wall.

He looks at the fractured cement in the sidewalk, splintering into the curb. Cars pass.

"Let's go inside," she says.

"All right," he says.

*

They sit in a dark booth near the back of the restaurant.

She has a drink. He has a drink.

He drinks his drink.

She looks at him.

Her glass has lipstick marks.

Her lipstick is not very red.

"It's nice," she says.

"Yeah," he says.

The booth is semi-circular. They sit in the middle, looking out at the restaurant.

There are many people. She lifts her glass.

Her arm is not as elegant as before.

Her arm is not as pale as before.

She drinks her drink and looks away.

"How is it," he says.

"All right," she says.

"Good."

"Yes."

The waiter comes. The waiter has a mustache and his hair is shiny.

He does not like the waiter.

They order.

They wait.

"San Francisco is a great town," she says.

"Is it?" he says.

"Better than Los Angeles."

"Is it?"

"I think it is."

He doesn't know. He doesn't miss Los Angeles.

He doesn't care for San Francisco.

"Doesn't it all seem the same," he says.

"Not really," she says.

He sighs and orders another drink.

He drinks his other drink.

They finish.

The waiter wants to know how the food was.

"It was fine," he says.

"Very good," she says.

They pay the bill. He pays the bill.

*

He is buzzed, but not drunk. He wanted to be drunk.

She only had one drink.

She holds his arm as they walk back down Market. It is very dark.

There is less traffic.

A sewer grate in the street is clogged with debris and garbage.

The streetlights hum. She clings to him.

He is annoyed.

He hates her. Sometimes.

He has been hating her more and more.

That's the liquor talking.

"That was nice," she says.

He says nothing. They walk back, down Market.

They head to Union Square.

"Let's look around the square. I bet it's nice at night," she says.

"Okay," he says.

They go into the square.

It is quiet. People sleep in doorways. The construction's gone silent. They walk towards the middle of the square.

"The Sir Francis Drake," she says. "You were right."

"Yeah," he says.

They sit down on a bench.

He looks up. There are no stars. Is it overcast? Or the city lights?

He can't see them.

He would like to see them.

"There aren't any stars," he says.

She looks up.

"No, there aren't," she says.

"We can't see them in LA either."

"So?"

"I guess it doesn't matter."

"You can see them sometimes."

"I guess."

Sine wave. What does that mean? It popped into his head. The words "sine wave".

"Sine wave," he says.

"What?" she says.

"Never mind."

She holds his hand.

"Let's go," he says.

They go.

*

The door across the hall is closed. He looks at it.

She looks at it.

She looks at him.

She looks at it again.

She looks at him again.

He looks away from it.

He opens their door.

She goes into the bathroom and closes the door.

He throws his coat on the floor.

He looks at the root protruding from the pile of sand.

There is no tree.

"There's no tree," he yells to her through the door.

No response.

He hears her running the water in the bathroom.

He takes his shoes off.

He picks up the ice bucket and takes off the plastic.

He pats his pockets.

He has the room key.

He leaves the room and walks down the hall.

*

The carpet smells.

The walls are beige. Hideous.

The ice machine is old. It says ICE on it. He pushes the bucket against the lever.

The machine rumbles.

Ice falls into the bucket.

He watches the ice fall into the bucket.

His hand is cold.

He looks up and the blonde from across the hall is standing there.

She wears a silk robe.

Her hair is done up and her makeup is perfect.

Her lips are very red.

"Hi," she says.

"Hi," he says.

"You're across the hall, right?"

"Yeah."

"Where you from?"

"LA."

"Oh, I love LA! I love Hollywood."

He nods. "What about you?"

"I'm from back east."

"Back east."

"Back east."

"What about your friend?" He saw them.

"She's from back east too."

She knows he saw them. She smiles.

He smiles.

They smile.

She pushes her bucket against the ice dispenser.

The machine rumbles.

"What's your name," he says.

"Why?" she says.

"I want to know."
"If I tell you, you'll forget it."
"No, I won't."
"Therese."
"Therese."
She smiles.
He puts his hand on her shoulder.
She looks at it.
He leans in and kisses her.
She kisses him back.
He holds his ice bucket.
She holds her ice bucket.
They kiss.
He feels her breast with his empty hand.
She moans.
He reaches into her robe and puts his hand between her legs.
She is wet. She is shaven.
"Therese," he says.
She moans.
He removes his hand and they kiss again.
"Goodnight," she says.
"Goodnight Therese," he says.
She walks back to her room and the door closes behind her.
He stands in front of the ice machine holding his bucket.
The ice drips.
*

More sawdust on the floor.
Or sand.
It's spilling out of the wall.
She lies in bed, her eyes open.
"Where were you," she says.
"Getting ice," he says.

She does not reply.

It smells like her lotion. Or shampoo. Or something.

He puts the ice down on the small table.

He takes one of the small plastic cups and scoops some ice out of the bucket.

He pours a bottled water into the cup.

She watches television.

He drinks the water.

She rolls over.

He chews the ice.

He crunches the ice in his teeth.

She cranes her head back towards him.

"Can you not do that?" she says.

"What?" he says.

"That. Chewing ice."

"Sorry."

He throws the cup in the trash.

He lays down next to her. She turns off the television.

It is dark. A sound comes through the walls.

A humming.

Some kind of reverberation.

An industrial sound.

"What is that?" he says.

"What is what?" she says.

"Can't you hear that?"

"Hear what?"

"Never mind."

"Where were you?"

"Getting ice."

She does not reply.

*

HORSES ON THE BEACH

Remember the time? Oh yes, I remember the time well. When was that? Many years ago and many years ago. Gnawing away, the hungry ghosts gnawing gnawing. Insubstantial devouring substantial. Fuel for the fire of the thousand thousand lives since passed. When was the time (Oh yes, I remember the time well,) when I felt the craven desire of this impulse like a simple scratching on the skin, away, when I was young. Remember the time? Oh yes, I remember the time well.

But it's not all memory. It can't be all memory. It can't be all ghosts, no. I haven't consigned my fire to the ghosts. In time. Maybe in time. But after so long there's so much memory and everything reminds. This place, no, it's this place, that's why I came here. To remember. I remember. I still remember, even not being here, I remember. But being here I remember better, yes, I remember better being here. There's a smell, there are sounds, there are things I remember well.

It's changed since then. The sea is still the same of course. The sea is always the same, but many things have been built up since. Many things have been built up and many things have been taken down taken down. But in the middle is the same space spreading out in all directions. In the middle there is a space. What goes in this space? I don't remember. Did I ask? I asked before and I can't remember what it was. Was there something that goes here? What was it? What goes in the space?

There was that time. I remember it well. Oh yes. We came here. His name was what was it? It was, well I remember him. We came here and he said to me look at the ocean. I remember he told me that. Look at the ocean and he said it that way and I looked, he said it and I looked. He smiled at me then and I can still remember it and the way it felt and was it that long ago but I still can think of it and smile too. I looked at the ocean (he said and I looked) and he kissed the back of my neck. And I closed my eyes and felt the sea breeze in my face and was it that long ago?

Things collected on the beach. There is the wood and there are the shells and wood and shells and things that have rolled in, many things, (so many things) but it comes together and on the beach it comes together, it makes this picture and I remember the way it came together. The salt water covers all that collects there and the salt itself collects and salt-whitened (all is salt-whitened) the way I remember it and there is metal sometimes and the bright orange dissolution in the salt bath rotting like the driftwood on the sand, rotting and dissolution and in this space that is what gathers (here in the middle) where the things are collected, that's what's here. That is what was here.

Then (was it so long ago) there were others. There are others now, but they are different. Or the others of then (I remember them well) became the others of now and the others of others, but then I can see them there on the beach. Many. I can still remember what happened then and it's happened before and it's happened since, but that time I can recall especially. But it gets difficult, oh yes, it gets difficult. Images and pieces and this and that and vaguely vaguely it comes into the clear.

There was a barrel. The barrel was almost full. The barrel had been filled nearly to the brim. The barrel was filled with liquid. (What was it?) Was it clear or was it dark? It could have been clear or dark. But there was a barrel.

There was that and I can remember it well, it was one of the first things I think of and I remember it, but this was before. This was before all the rest.

Well, after he kissed my neck (he said, I looked, he kissed, I closed my eyes) I turned and looked at him. He had this look. The look I saw and have seen but hadn't seen until I saw it then. He took my hand and we walked down to the beach. Yes I saw it all then (it lingers) all and the salt decay.

He stopped me short. He held my hand. He took my hand and stopped me short. It was then that I first saw them. (Oh, how the hungry ghosts devour.) They were brown and white and spotted and specked and I had never (my dear) I had never seen them, or seen it, yes it was a day of many firsts. They were big and loud and came forward quickly, so quickly, and he squeezed my hand and I looked at him and he said to me do you like horses and I said to him I don't know. Yes I did and he laughed and I can see him laughing now like he is here, he must be here, no this was so long, was it that long, it was so long, but I can still see him laughing.

The horses trotted along the shore, brown ones, white ones. We took a spot up on the cliff and lay in the sand and we watched and he had my hand and we saw them trot along and the men led them down and down toward the debris.

The horses lined up and the people were down there, but we couldn't see their faces, we were too far away, but he squeezed my hand, yes I remember it well. He said, and I can remember him saying, there is a race and I said oh and he said yes there is a race and I said why is there a race. He laughed (we still held hands).

It started (this was when it happened) the race started and the horses began down the beach. They flew along the beach and it seemed impossible, ridiculous that their spindly legs could carry them but they bent and pushed and they moved so quickly so quickly. They went down the beach and right as they reached the turn (the insubstantial) he kissed me and I can remember it (the substantial). It was the first kiss. The horses came back they were so close, they were so fast, and then (this is when it happened) then the one, a brown one, he was all brown, he stepped in something, it was a hole, there was a hole. There are holes in the beach. He stepped and I saw his leg go in maybe down to the knee and he was going so fast and he flipped forward and the man on top got thrown and the horse fell over and I could hear the crack and my god my god I said and I still hear that crack I can still hear it because it's never stopped cracking.

The horse lay on the beach, writhing terribly. The man came running, this other man, I don't know who he was, he came running so fast he knocked over that barrel and it busted when it hit the side and it was like this horse and it busted open and the liquid inside oozed out and down the sand slowly. This dark liquid (it was dark, I mean, it could have been clear, in the barrel, for all I know, but outside, it was clearly dark.)

He held me then and told me not to look, but I saw and I didn't want to, but I did want to and I did and he held me so close and I watched the horse, it was so helpless, I watched him. They helped the man, the man who was thrown. Then they tried to help the horse, but they couldn't help him and something had happened and I saw the man shaking his head, looking at the horse and I heard him say poor creature and I thought poor creature and he held me tightly and I said why and he did not laugh.

There was a time. Was it so long ago? I was just a girl then. Yes it was long. But I remember some things very well, like that time then with that man. When I come here, I try not to too often, but it happens. But that was many years ago, many years ago and the ghosts are never satisfied. The insubstantial demands the substantial and memory is so powerful. Maybe it comes with age and the blessings of a full life (it had been many years ago) but the demands of the past, they demand, and it's a strong pull back into that space (what goes in that space, the space in the middle?) and the deluge of what was comes back with all the salt-white salt-decay and tangled wood and running wild and the kiss of that man (the first kiss) and it all blurs together like a torrent against my fire, like the orange dissolution, like the craven howling ghosts, like the fragile tenuous barrel, like the days and years between, like the horses on the beach.

HOW TO BUILD A TABLE

1

He stands tall in the garage. The garage, where all the tools are.
The tools belong to him and one day, he says, the tools will
belong to me. For now, I don't touch the tools. The taboo of the
tools covers them like a curtain.
Blades and pincers and smashers and knobs and buttons and
gauges and the taboo of the tools
and he stands tall.
At times, after dinner, he goes into the garage. He stays there
all night. I hear the rhythmic pounding or scratching or sawing
or
I hear the noises from the garage, when he's in the garage. I
don't watch him. He uses the tools. I can hear the sound of the
tools when he uses them, but I have not seen him use the tools.
One time I GET THE HELL OUT OF HERE and that was that.

He eats his dinner with his elbows on the table. He eats his
dinner with a cold grimace. The food is good, as far as I know it,
and mother has worked hard to prepare it. He eats it with a cold
grimace and his elbows on the table, staring back. When he
finishes, he wipes his mouth hurriedly with his napkin and, at
times, goes into the garage when he's done.

He always smells like wood. It's a good smell, as far as I know it,
and it smells like the fire he makes in the winter when our
breath comes out in clouds as we lay in our beds. It is the smell
of wood. He works with the wood. He works with the wood in

the garage and he works with the wood at work. There is a large lumber mill in our town. That's where he works. He goes there, in the mornings, after he eats his breakfast (cold grimace, elbows up), then takes his lunch pail,
It is tin, it is metal, the lunch pail.
and goes out the door towards the mill. He walks. We don't have a car. A lot of people around here don't have cars. Some have cars. We don't.

At the mill he works with the wood. I don't know what he does with the wood. I haven't seen. I've heard the mill. Everyone hears the mill. I've smelled the wood. Everyone smells the wood. But only he smells *like* the wood.

At times he talks about the mill. Always bad. THIS JOB IS KILLING ME he spoons his potatoes into his mouth and EVER SINCE BILL HENNY LEFT I dabs his mouth with his napkin but WHAT THE HELL WOULD YOU KNOW and then he stands up and JESUS CHRIST goes into the garage.
He goes into the garage and resumes his work.
He goes. I am trying to say, He goes, let's look.
He goes to the mill. At the mill he works with the wood. After the mill he comes home and THE MILL IS GOING STRAIGHT TO HELL and then he goes into the garage and resumes his work with the wood.
He goes from woodwork to woodwork he goes from. He goes STRAIGHT TO HELL, I TELL YOU into the garage.

He has asked me into the garage. COME HERE I WANT TO SHOW YOU SOMETHING.

He asked. I have never seen. I have never. And. The taboo of the tools covers them like a curtain.

I AM GOING TO SHOW YOU HOW TO BUILD A TABLE stained jean overalls, he wore them out painting when she said that the house needed painting and he I AM GOING TO SHOW YOU put on the overalls and took up the paint can and took up the brush and COME OVER HERE AND LOOK AT THIS

He shaved. He always shaves. I've never seen him with a beard. DO YOU KNOW THE WOOD? He smells like cigarettes and he looks like cigarettes (it is something I would say again and again and again) and THERE ARE ONLY TWO JOBS IN THIS TOWN his thin gray hair, greasy and matted and IT'S WHAT A HARD DAY'S WORK LOOKS LIKE he would THE MILL often take a AND THE TOBACCO FARMS small tin can from his back pocket and YOU DON'T WANT TO WORK THE FARMS
apply the paste to
WITH THE BLACKS
his hair.

NOW LISTEN UP
His undershirt is dirty and stained. Stray black hairs from his body poke through the fabric. Sweat beads on his arms. The smell of his breath NOW LISTEN UP.

2
A TABLE IS A PLANE WITH FOUR LEGS DO YOU UNDERSTAND
the writhing the wriggling the worms on the hook he took you fishing he took you out to the bridge to the place to the river to the lake to the fishing he took you and he pierced the worm with the hook and threw it down into the river off the bridge and he

took you but you remember the writhing the wriggling of the
fish on the hook of the worm on the hook on the hook on the
hook of when he took you on the hook
THIS IS HOW YOU BUILD A TABLE
cold of the snow on your feet without boots and the other
children without boots and you played outside and the mud on
your feet on the floor and the fire and the woodfire burning
burning burning and the washing of the mud off the feet and the
shivering the anticipating the knowing and not knowing when it
snowed and you could smell the Christmas food cooking and
cooking and burning and the snow on the ground in the white of
the way out to the path where the dog on the stake froze that
night when it snowed and the look on its face when you found
THIS IS HOW TO OPERATE A TABLESAW DO YOU UNDERSTAND
the little coffin when he died and the knot in the wood that yes
of course he built the coffin and there was a knot and he always
threw out the knots but he left it on the plane on the side on the
coffin the little coffin that she put his little body in when you
were little too and nobody cried and you had heard that people
should cry that there would be crying but there was no crying
just the cold grimace and the knot in the wood as the little wood
box was lowered into the little hole in the ground and the
ground was still frozen and you wanted to stop it but he lowered
the coffin into the ground and he lowered it into the ground
YOU MUST SAND THE WOOD UNTIL IT IS SMOOTH
and after all that the one night with the nightmares and you
couldn't sleep and you couldn't wait and all in your bed were the
phantasms and the souls you had seen slip away and the empty
mistakes and the ephemeral dust and you snuck down the hall in
the hopes you could join them but you got to the hallway and
heard something happening and you looked in their bedroom
and saw something happening and you looked in the bedroom

and you looked and you saw something happening you saw
something happening you saw something you saw something
you saw you saw saw saw saw

3

He put his hand around mine and said, "Son, this is how you use
the handsaw. Be sure to have a firm grip. Be sure the wood is
secured in the vice. Always pencil a line across the wood so you
get a straight cut. Make sure the teeth of the saw are sharp
before you start and be sure to collect the sawdust for later,
you never know when you're going to need it."

"Thanks, dad. I will," I said. He smiled and patted me on the
head. He stood so tall in the garage over me and I knew he built
most of our furniture and that woodworking was his passion. It
was such a thrill, I felt so alive and grown up and so much love
for him. He took off his work gloves and hung them up on the
high peg in the garage that I could not reach.

"Now don't use any of my tools unless I say so and come out
here with you. I'll teach you all about them but there's no rush.
Now, I think I can smell your mother's dessert. What do you say
we go in and eat," he said.

"Sounds great, dad. It sounds just great," I said.

He patted me on the head again and we went inside.

He had shown me how to build a table. How to build a table.
How to build a table. *how to build a table how to build a table*
how to build a table HOW TO BUILD A TABLE HOW TO BUILD A
TABLE HOW TO BUILD A TABLE

QUESTIONS OF SCALE

As I sat, entrenched in my business as usual, I thought I heard a faint buzzing from a distant corner of my office. I paid it little heed and continued my work. I can only express the importance of the work I do with great difficulty, and I can't even begin to put into words its details. In any case, the work must get done. Each day I begin anew, dutifully eking out the tasks assigned to me, carefully inspecting my work, double checking it even, to ensure its accuracy. Again, the buzzing. What a distraction! My work, this burden I carry, must get done, and I am distracted by a petty annoyance.

I decided it would be more efficient to deal with the buzzing now and work quickly in peace than to try and continue working with the buzzing distraction interrupting my thoughts. My cursory examination of the corner from which the buzzing seemed to come revealed nothing. However, the corner was in shadow and I could hardly make out its contents, if there were any.

It had been a long, long time since I had paid attention to this corner, or even this whole side of my office. My work demands my strict attention and I cannot be bothered with constant inspection of every inch of my domain. That said, upon returning to it now in pursuit of this miniscule bother, I found it a rather dull and desolate corner, bereft of that which made the remainder of my office not only tolerable, but enjoyable. Yet this corner existed, had existed, and lacked only my gaze upon it to come into the fore. But soon, without subsequent buzzing, I dismissed the corner, its indeterminate contents, and returned to my work.

Having hardly started at my work again in the comfort of my desk in the center of my office, the buzzing began again in earnest. This time, I jumped from my desk and raced to the corner. Staring intently, I attempted to make out the buzzing's source. Again: nothing. But as I stood there, hovering over the corner, bent in two, with my own shadow blocking the light by which I saw, I thought I noticed a very faint movement, the movement of a dark object within darkness, hardly reflecting the immense light that flooded the rest of the room. I knelt, which I hesitated doing without probable cause, as the joints of my knees give me trouble and bringing myself up to my full height once again would require a great deal of effort and perhaps even pain.

Sure enough, I had not knelt in vain. In the very deepest recesses of the corner, down in the rug fibers, fluttered an infinitesimally small fly. It moved in place, not flying, but flapping its tiny, fragile wings, twisting its body one direction, then another, producing the frustrating buzz that had plagued me this entire morning.

My first instinct was to strike it viciously and forever end its grotesque existence. But, as I watched it writhe absently, a mere speck to my eyes, I began to feel that perhaps crushing the life out of this fly was not the answer. I had killed many flies before, and other insects, had they wandered into my sight, and I would kill many more. But now, I only stared, watching in silence as this fly moved erratically in the darkness amid the chemically treated synthetic hairs of the carpet.

From where had this fly come? It lived in my office, but I couldn't recall letting it in. It came from somewhere, obviously, but I didn't remember where. What really puzzled me and stayed my hand from its murderous descent was why the fly behaved as it did.

My work demands logic, precision, clear causality, mathematics... This fly, beating its wings against itself, moved at random, with no purpose, with no obvious goal. Was it only a question of scale? Because the fly could fit into the tip of my little finger with room to spare, did it follow that I could not relate to its being? Or did the fly lack being, as I used the term, and only mechanically follow simple instinctual commands, this particular fly having had its circuits crossed or cut or tangled in a way that made its usually sensible programming go haywire? Neither of these hypotheses satisfied me, for if the fly lacked being, where did one draw the line between being and non-being? And if the fly had being, but operated strictly on instinct, what type of creature would that make? There would be no difference between a fly acting on base instinct and a rock traveling through space with a certain trajectory and speed. In that scenario, the line between being and non-being simply did not exist. I was sure that experts in some field knew the answer, or at least more details about how a fly worked, but I, being a lay person in these matters, struggled against my own ignorance, new hypotheses emerging by the second.

I observed this fly, questioning why I could observe this fly, think about it, reflect upon it, abstract it to the concept of A Fly, while its pathetic faculties could hardly utilize the minimal amount of information provided by its genetics, if that's how it worked. How did the fly experience life? What did it mean to see the world through kaleidoscope eyes, to flap transparent wings, to stick the snout into a pile of excrement for sustenance, to buzz eclectic without hope of understanding, save an imperfect understanding by other flies, if indeed any could understand another?

And then why? Why exist as a fly? Perhaps the fly didn't know it existed. It lacked the observed observer of higher intelligence. Or perhaps its experiences were so different from mine that I was incapable of understanding it on my terms. Perhaps time seemed to pass much more slowly to a fly. Each second ticked away as for me a year would pass. Perhaps undetectable attributes gave its life meaning and interest. Some alien system of signification, so far missed by me, scattered through its dingy microcosm, filled the fly's world as the various expressions of my kind filled mine. Perhaps I projected my own feelings and thoughts onto this little speck, vicariously filling myself by filling it. The fly buzzed in agitation. What agitated it? Or was agitation my word, my experience, wholly foreign to this disgusting insect? It desperately buzzed, so quickly together did the pulses, that to my ears seemed a contiguous sound, come, that I ascribed desperation to its almost certainly meaningless flailing.

I had to turn away. I turned away in revulsion and horror. My urge to crush its existence returned. The buzzing had escalated from a minor annoyance to a pestilent intrusion, each individual click an expression of irrational and pointless being. I looked out the window of my office, where the light poured in from its source. But the buzzing in the darkness continued. My mind kept showing me the ill lit dance of the pathetic fly in the corner, lilting to and fro, its spindly legs turning deftly while its lidless eyes stared out in every direction.

Could it see me? Was the fly aware of my presence? If I swatted at it, it would dodge, but that only proved reflex to imminent danger. Did the fly recognize me as a continuous whole, a sentient creature, a separate entity? Or am I, as I see myself, wholly abstracted to the fly, who, because of insufficient mental powers, insufficient visual powers, insufficient comprehension, or any other limitation of its physical being, could not understand that I am a creature like it, save of a much higher order? When I hunched over it, looming above its entire universe, did it fear its death at my hand? When I stood, with difficulty, and retreated to my desk, did the fly feel relief? Did it know I had spared its life? Or did it conclude from its continued existence that I never was there to destroy it in the first place?

I could not focus on my work. I could not sit peacefully in my chair. My ears resounded with the buzzing of this fly and I wanted to crush it crush it crush it until silence once again prevailed. Silence, the natural order, brought me great happiness. This impertinent fly sought to steal my peace of mind, my comfort, my ability to continue my work, with its irrational noise! How dare it have the audacity to intrude on a superior creature like me with its meaningless existence? I could not leave my office. I could not abandon my work. I could not go on like this.

Then, an amazing thing happened. The fly left its corner and flew in a nearly straight line towards the window. At last, progress! This I could understand. Spending its whole life grappling with itself in a dark corner, it had finally decided to seek out the light and perhaps escape. I watched intently as the fly buzzed its way quickly over to the window pane. It buzzed frantically, desperately, to my ears, and flew up against the glass pane again and again. Ah, fly, could you only understand the transparency of glass... But it only continued its assault, drawn by the light, repeatedly flying into the window, buzzing, faster and faster, slamming itself into the glass, buzzing, louder and louder, trying different angles, different parts of the glass surface, buzzing, higher and higher, again and again and again SMASH into the glass pane, SMASH into the glass pane, SMASH into the glass pane, and to no avail at all. Could it not see the folly in this, its inability to affect, even in the slightest, its macro-environment? I saw it all so clearly, the helplessness of this tiny, strange entity, smashing its foolish self against an immovable obstacle, all in the hopes of attaining a distant light that it could neither reach nor understand, a light that would immolate it in seconds with indifferent alacrity. It buzzed and buzzed and continued to buzz.

I should have opened the window, perhaps, though behind the glass was a screen, through which the fly could never have passed, and which I was unwilling to remove for its sake. Would not allowing it a touch of fresh air have been yet another torture it endured? It wasn't my place, anyway, from what I could recall, to assist this creature in its futile struggle, nor would it have helped. And even if I did help this one fly, millions or billions or trillions more writhed elsewhere, pleading for succor that would never come.

With a final assault, the fly rammed itself into the glass pane, fluttered in the air for a moment, and fell lifeless to the floor. The buzzing ceased. Quiet filled the office. I gazed upon the inert remains of the fly, awkwardly lying on its side, and for all I knew, no longer troubled by its world or mine, whatever they may have been. The fly corpse disgusted me, but I remained still, despite my urge to sufficiently pad my fingers with tissue and move its husk from my office floor to the trash can. I sat calmly, quietly in the calm and quiet.

I left my office, much work undone, sure that something would remove the fly from my floor before Monday. It had grown dark; I had stared at the fly for a very long time. I left my building and felt the cold, fresh air on my skin. Everything stood immobile and hushed. The quiet extended far out into the clear sky above, descended far down into the cracks of the icy sidewalk below my feet. I yawned loudly, stretching my arms outward, my elbows clicking as they popped, then yawned again. My neck craned towards the sky, and I was able to barely make out the wispy glow of the Milky Way against the surrounding blackness.

O MY SON

I remember he came into the study and grabbed that book and his little hands wrapped around it and the book was so big in his little hands and he pulled it down and, flesh of my flesh, he wanted the book and I didn't let him have the book, but because he was so little and too little to understand, but I didn't read it to him when I could have read it to him anyway and even if he didn't understand it, I could have read it to him and then much later, when he could have understood it, he didn't read it because we both forgot, but it was so long ago and it's only now coming back and I remembered right away, right when it was too late and my blood, too late now for anything and how can I go on when, my blood, how can I go on?

We did I think, I say we did, but we only know what we know and how much we know is only the parts and pieces that we know, but we think, I think, we did the best we could, we never always, we tried, we wanted to do the best we could, there are times we could have done better, but it all moves so slow until it's over and I always told him I was proud, I could have told him more often though and we never said I love you because it wasn't our way, but I know he knew, I think he knew, we only know what we know and I think he knew, but now it's too late and I can't tell him and no one can tell him ever again and if she were here she would speak those words to his stone, but I cannot.

But she's gone and she's been gone and truth be told, my blood,

I'm glad she is, my love, I'm glad she is gone, because if she was here, this would be the end all over again, and much worse, much worse, much worse, because cancer isn't a flame in the wind to this and to see it all over again and now it's too late for both of them and I am a man, just a man, who wanted to be a man, who wanted, I thought, I thought I knew, but I can't and if she were here, I can't even imagine the tears and the silence and it would be too much and even now just the thought of her being like me, here, after this, is too much too bear, far too much to bear and

How much of this scotch is left and I've drank so much and it's sat in this decanter now for years, even when he was young, even when she was here, I've had this here and now I drink it and assimilate it and soon it will be like he and her, gone and too late and never again constituent and it's gone and she's gone and now he's gone and how can I continue on after all of this and keep asking myself here in this library where the book he took off the shelf so many years ago calls my name from its place on the shelf and I should have read it to him, I should have read it to him, I should have.

But he read so many of them and none of them were this one and all the ones he read weren't this one, or even if they were, they weren't this one, because at that time I didn't read it to him and now there are shelves of books and all shelves of books he won't read either and the candle of the dust burns out, or is that how it goes, mostly I just read them here and there before bed, even before the cancer, in bed with a light, reading here and there and something like the candle of the dust, but probably not, I don't remember much except the candle of the dust and I thought of that too, as soon as I heard, and his little hand holding that book and when I told him no, but I couldn't tell him yes, at the time it seemed like the no was the yes for the long term and there were a lot of nos, so I don't know why this one, but maybe one more yes or one more no, but how could I have known then, how could I know now, there's no knowing any more than the candle of the dust burns out or however it goes, it was something like that though, it was something like it.

Maybe she's right, the girl he was with, they had been together a while now I think, maybe his longest one, but I don't know for sure, which only proves what she said, when she said it there with his body there and said it in front of all those people and cried and cried and she really did love him and she loved him with that burning love that people know is love, but I loved him too, in my way, and maybe that's not enough, maybe it's not right, but I did love him, no matter what she said, or any of them said, and maybe my love is a little colder, maybe it's cold, but it's love and no matter how cold it is, it's still love and when she told me that and I had to leave and I couldn't stay, but I could see she loved him and that's why I left, because she really did.

And the little one asking my son, my other son, my only son now, my god, my only son now, asking him why and asking him why and his cherub face asking the why of the void and my son, my other son, my only son now, telling him to shush, to quiet down, but I wanted to know too and I want to know now and, if I ever learn, I will tell you, my flesh too, my only flesh, the only line left to me now, the only line left and I love you too, in my way, I love you too and your father, in my way, in my way I love you.

It's all mystery, always shrouded inside this silence, this absence, this darkness and no answers, no questions, just this vague amorphous haze and these chest clenching longings for that which is taken and gone forever and always, hopeless, but still yearning onward, like an animal, like without experience of the grand event, like still looking at his face motionless in the coffin, or like him young and happy on our vacation to my mother's house in North Carolina and him with his feet in the black sand, asking about the piles of lumber by the mill and how I used to work there and him sitting and asking and wondering and being and now no more and me still here, grey and here.

I knew nothing at his age, his frozen age, his suspended youth, but I knew nothing, no, it is no greatness to die young and immortalize, yes I have lost some verve, but all I have learned and seen and felt and he never will, but he had his life and remember he brought home girls, but still just learning, only beginning, and my own blood and my pride and washed out rain water pulling me down under the door into the street and into the gutter and so much I never told him, as was my duty, but I always thought there would be time and child of my flesh who spoke in my voice, who hated and loved me, who missed his mother so many nights, and trying to explain and justify and say that God works in his ways and speaking into the silence, always without echo, voice falling flat and empty words popping under the slightest touch, flitting fairy fragments and now gone forever and no more justification and no more lies and no more speech, just these few pictures now and my frozen family forever.

But flesh why, but blood why, why, I've asked myself many

times, many times, and what could I have done, but what could I have done and maybe if she hadn't died of cancer, if she had been here to give the love I couldn't speak, to speak the words I couldn't feel, if she had been here, he would be here, but I don't know, I just think, but maybe even not and I haven't been much a part of his life these last years and now it's too late and we were distant and maybe have been for as long as he was a man, which was so short, he had so much time and now it's too late and this scotch is almost dry and the book calls from the shelf and my blood, my blood, my flesh, my son, too late.

A DISGRUNTLED MAN CROSSES THE STREET

Jeffrey steps down off of the curb.

God lives in the swaying trees, like a voice calling out over the streets, like the garbage accumulating in the gutter. There is no God. There is nothing new in the invisible wind. There is. There is not. There is nothing new. The ants crawl over one another in a great pile in concrete sidewalk cracks. They crawl and crawl over each other, delicate leg upon leg, crawling, a black pile. Along the edges, the strays wander aimlessly across the cement until they are crushed, or starved, or return, finally, to the crowd. The pile pulses like a black artery in a concrete body. There is organization and order and symmetry and poetry and God. There is no organization, nor order, nor symmetry, nor poetry, nor God.

Jeffrey, you look up now. You've been down too long. You look up. Look up. You, look up. Shut up.

Mown grass stink. Piles and piles of the blades of the grass. The bodies move to and fro, passing and coming, silent. How do you explain the silence? How do you explain the silence to those who hear music all the time, while you turn and scream and have nothing and see everything and press forward, one foot in front of the other, automatic, deathly, begging for a misstep. But no misstep comes.

Jeffrey, you are too careful for that. You would never fall. You'll never fall.

Dampen the awareness. Just turn down the brightness a little, is all I ask, and why are there piles of ants between the concrete blocks of the sidewalks and why do they crawl and why is it this shifting black mass in lines that I see, but is otherwise ignored? Just turn it down a little bit. Just a little bit.

Is that a tremor in your hand? Too much or too little caffeine or sugar. Too much or too little exercise. Nervous, anxious? Are you anxious, Jeffrey?

It's nothing. I just need to get where I am going.

Swallow your voice like bile. There is nothing and no one to rebel against. You can file your grievances at the head office. Is that man laughing? Is he laughing at you? They walk by and you see in the lines of their faces your ceiling staring and the silence and the separation.

After all, it's such a tenuous grasp on experience. Indescribable, incommunicable. But is it really happening? Cut off at the stem, growing in the air with a last gasp. Photosynthesizing the energy of a perpetual stellar explosion in the shadow of your own death, your withering bud blossoming into irrelevancy.

Jeffrey, go lie down in that field and die. In the tall grass. You want to die.

What is the difference between life and death and what does it matter to those people who refuse to look into the gaping chasm between them over which we hover? You only have to look down once and your gaze is fixed forever.

Jeffery, do you wish you never knew that all the questions you've ever asked have gone unanswered? Do you wish you never even knew to ask them? Jeffrey?

Fundamental questions need be asked. Is it abnormal to ask one's self whether the macrocosmic differences trump the microcosmic similarities when putting on one's clothes in the morning, standing before a mirror, adjusting one's hair or inspecting one's figure? Am I abnormal? Is normalcy a mask we wear collectively to assuage our own fears through mutual validation?

Jeffrey, if you were to die in a field, your body would be rent to pieces by creatures large and small. Fear the fragmentation of your own flesh. Jeffrey, you would never let the birds and rodents eat your eyes. You would never.

Hahaha they call you crazy if you reach out and grab a stranger and shake them and yell in their face ISN'T IT HORRIBLE, ISN'T IT ALL SO TERRIBLE? even though it is, and you know it, and they know it, but to acknowledge it is criminal, insane. I'm not insane. Just grab someone, anyone, let them feel the pressure of your grip, force them to acknowledge your existence as a discrete, sentient being, and demand they acknowledge the horror of everything we have ever known or of which we can even conceive. Haha.

Jeffrey, if you did that you'd get arrested. They'd put you away.

It isn't my fault that the ants crawl over each other in a black, shifting pile. If we could see atoms, if we could see protons and neutrons and electrons, all we would see is a countless, swirling mass of particles, crossing in and out from each other, attracting, repelling, swirling like a black wind, forever. No people, no sidewalks, no ants, no trees, no grass, none of these arbitrary delineations we make with our macrovision would even occur to us. It would be only the unintelligible ebbs and flows of an ocean of matter, swirling endlessly. There would be no life, no death, just the endless procession of atoms, transforming and flowing gracefully into each other. This is a picture of the world in which we live. We just can't see it. To hell with all this damnable whatness.

Jeffrey, what are you talking about?
I'm talking about a mask of God.
Jeffrey. There is no God. Jeffrey, there is no God.

A mask of somethingness over a face of nothingness. Every blade of grass subsists as a solar parasite. There is nothing that feeds on nothing. Every sun feeds off its own stomach. Self-devouring titans. Gnashing their teeth to better auto-cannibalize. The furnace roars until its fuel supply grows scant. Then its mask collapses on its own hollow and it explodes in every direction at the speed of light.

Every force attracts and repels. The mechanics of the universe don't fascinate me, only my ability to perceive them. Only my futile struggle to inscribe them in a universe of meaning. The difference between this universe and my perception of it is the infinite void of anxiety, despair, and hope. Only the unknown is precious. Monster of desire wormed into an apple heart. There's garbage along the concrete walls. A metal rail slides down the ramp, and there the garbage rests, blown about, around, and scattered. Concrete. Metal. Plastic. Glass. Garbage.

Jeffrey, where are you going?

Forward, always, not from choice or even recognizable impetus, but caught in a current. Born into an undertow and dragged out to sea to flounder for my time and drown in empty obscurity. While around me cars drive back and forth, back and forth, buying groceries. Sitting water attracts swarms. Birthgrounds. Back and forth, going to the store. Grocery store aisles make me want to die. Too bright, too intense. "Someone" turn down the horror of abundance. (No answer.) Blunt my oversharp point on a diamond hard barrier. Forever compartmentalizing. Closing doors to never re-open them or scavenge about their ruinous contents. If every moment we've ever experienced is stored in our memory and only our recall is imperfect then we should be grateful not to experience a terrible perfection. Hail the virtue of forgetfulness. Float down that river in an inner tube, sunglasses on, tolerating the present only through the fantasy shading of our lenses, without worry, without knowledge of the future, without doubt. And onward to nothingness, in which we need not fear or question. Into the inanimate, the eternal, the uncaring, unconscious dispersion of our grotesque energy into the vast cosmos until we stretch so thin and mix so thoroughly that we can finally claim the bounty of annihilation.

You don't know death, Jeffrey. You are afraid.
I don't know death. I am afraid.
Jeffrey steps up onto the curb.

THE LARGEST CROSS

COME SEE
THE SECOND LARGEST CROSS
IN THE WESTERN HEMISPHERE
PRAYER SERVICE
THE STATIONS OF THE CROSS
FAMILY FRIENDLY FUN
ONLY IN TEXAS

I
(scratch, scratch scratch)

Wiping the dust.
Wiping the dust from the thief.
Wiping the dust from the thief on His right.

The wind blow up fierce this morning. The wind blowing up. It
blow up the dust and scatter it here, there, on me, in me.
Wiping. I wiping off his face. I wiping the dust off his face. There
more. There more dust. I wiping it off too, the more, and then
there still more. Then there the other thief. Then there still
more.

I clean both thieves and the Lord.
I clean them with this cloth.
I wipe the dust from their faces.
I wipe it with this cloth.

We in the shadow of the cross now. It spreading out across this
field the way it does. It hot out too. In the shadow ain't so hot.

We in the shadow of the cross. The dust bad. They always saying the dust bad for you. It get in your lungs. The dust build up in your lungs. You breathe it. They say. Plenty a work in the office, they say. Plenty of work. Ain't much for office work, I say Ain't much for it. Rather it in the dust.

That one there, the one there, the one over there, he said, he said something like, he said something like, 'Lord don't forget me when you go up into Your Kingdom.' He wished it and then got taken up and the other one got sent below. It in the book. I read it.

-Rudy, Hey Rudy! he call out to me.

He walking up the platform now, blowing all over in the wind, like I must look. It a sight. I must a sight myself. I must. But him, in them black robes or whatever he calls them, and his starched white collar, blasted with the dust. It blowing on him, over him, same as me. Blasting him.

-Morning.

-Morning there Rudy, how's it going then? Stations look real good, real good. Why don't you come on inside for a bit and grab some breakfast. Everyone else is already inside.

I nod at him, though I ain't that hungry. I do not feel hungry. He looking at me now with those eyes he has. He looking at me now with those eyes. I haven't finished cleaning up the statues yet. He looking at me now hard, real hard.

If it rain later on, it wash off all this anyway and it won't have meant nothing to even bother. I ain't quite that hungry, but I going anyway. It won't have meant nothing. I ain't hungry. I going anyway, down into the building. I going down anyway.

(scratch, scratch)

They already got breakfast all laid out and they all sitting there already eating, sitting and eating, sitting, eating. They got breakfast all laid out. No Mr. Day. No Ms. Bernice. The rest already there, sitting, eating.

Eggs. Grits. Potatoes. Sausage. Ham. Rolls. Toast. Orange Juice. Coffee.

I don't drink coffee, though. I do not.

Long and them already all sitting there eating. Laughing bout something. Laughing. Sometimes he look at me with a meanness. Sometimes he look at me. Just look down and they go away. Just looking down. That look bred into a boy. Bred into him. Eggs. He that old Mr. Day's boy. Went off to college and all, I heard. It usually beat into them, but sometime it come about just through the blood. Potatoes. He heft stuff around here now, though. Him and those old boys there, hefting it around all day and working on the truck. They move the stuff around all right. Ham. They move it around all right. Toast.

Orange juice.

Maureen pour the orange juice. It her hand on the pitcher and she smiling when she pour it. It poured into the glass from her arm, lifting it, and she smiling as she does it. She smile at me a bit. She pouring the orange juice. She smile at me. She Long's wife. She his wife. She smile at me. She pour my orange juice.

-Morning there Rudy, she say. How ya doin'?

-All right, I suppose. I got the stations mostly wiped down, though there a few I ain't got, but I reckon if it rain later on it ain't gonna matter to have bothered now. How ya'll doing? How little Molly doing?

(scratch, scratch)

-We're good. Molly's good.

(scratch, scratch, scratch, scratch)

She smile at me. Father Sal waiting for his orange juice. I smile, or make to smile, and turn away. She very nice.

There are three tables.
There are three tables in the office.
Long and the boys, that Si and that Don, got one of them.

LONG LOOKING AT ME

Sal got another, but he got his bible out and he likely busy and not wanting any disturbing while he working out his sermon. He don't want no bother.

The last table got that Doc Conroy on it, with his bird eyes and bird nose and bird brow and looking through his book like he ain't even here. I set down by him, quiet, and start to eat. I taste the food and I chew it. I ain't that hungry.

-Rudolph. he say. He call me Rudolph.

-Doc. I call him Doc. Most folk call him Doc.

He keep on reading.
I keep on eating.

The light looking a touch strange. The light coming in from the window. The windows in the office high up and wide. The light coming in from them a little strange.

I fixing to get up and put my plate away and in come that little Molly, running around like mad. She IT SCRATCHING running around and laughing and IT TREMBLING wearing a little

scratch
a little dress that Maureen
tremble
must have got her last time they gone into town.

She look awfully cute.

-Hey there, Miss Molly. I say.

LONG LOOKING AT ME (I feel the embers of his eyes in the thick of my neck and I scratch it like scratch it and scratch at it peeling off the itch of his stare)

-Hiya, Rudy! she say. Ya'll already eat?

I look at my empty plate and IT EMPTY
I HAVE EATEN IT ALL
I nod and try to smile like
the way folks do

-Yes ma'am, just finished. You runnin' a little late, ain't you?

(scratch, scratch
it in me it in me it in me it in me
scratch)

-Yeah, I was getting pretty. Mama bought me this dress and did up my hair so I was making sure it was perfect before presenting myself.

LONG LOOKING
SHE GETTING PRETTY
getting pretty getting pretty getting pretty
did up her hair getting pretty
presenting herself getting pretty
getting pretty getting getting getting
pretty pretty
pretty

-Molly. he say from cross the room. LONG Molly, cmere. he say.

HE LOOKING AT ME

As he speak.

Not speaking to me but looking at me and looking at me, but his words not for me, but his eyes speak too and to me they speak to me and the itch of the embers of his eyes speak to me too.

SCRATCH SCRATCH SCRATCH
SHE SKIPS AND DANCES OVER TO HIM

-What I tell you about being late? he say, finally looking at her and speaking to her and I feeling a drop of sweat now and I wiping it away. I wiping it off.

-You know better'n that. Can't be running round here by yourself. It ain't safe. he say.

-But Daddy, I know everybody here.

-Don't talk back. Do what I tell you. Your ma'll worry if you're by yourself.

-Listen to your Daddy, baby. Don't be running round. Maureen say.

I listening and hearing the eyes and the voices and looking and trying not to look and to scratch the itch, but I feel it and if it rain today it won't be for nothing and it all set to a slow boil and coming up over the top and sides with some kind of abundance.

LOOK AWAY
GOD
LOOK AWAY

I on my feet and don't even know how I did and I feel the daggers of the embers of the eyes in my back and wish they could bleed me from all this bramble confusion, like I was on the table and bled it all out and make just like new and start it again and GOD now I see Sal there and he looking at me, waiting like, and I don't know what I should

-I said you need something, Rudy? he say.

-Uh. Sorry to bother you, Sal, just wanted to know what all you like me to do this morning.

He close that Bible on that red bookmark and there all kinds of notes and highlighting and things inside it and I can't make out his tiny crumped scrawl, but I did see it in there around the block printed words of the Lord in that book and he push up his reading glasses on his nose and looking at me with the eyes of a kind I never did feel, not like the embers, and I am not burned here, but he look at me all the same and I would almost want more the violent burning than his calm kindness.

-We're gonna have sermon at ten. It's what, round eight now? I don't reckon there's much to be done before then. Take some time to yourself, if you want.

time
to yourself

-All right then, thanks. I say.

-You can always read this. he say and hold up his bible.

I nod and inside hold down a laugh that bubble up and would come out a cry if it ever escaped, but it never will as long as I live and the

(scratch, scratch)
and the derisive
I CAN HEAR IT
and the penitent
DEAFENING
and if it rain
won't have mattered
none
anyway.

II
I like the feel of this book. There's a smoothness to the leather and a heavy texture to the pages that reinforce its weight. It's not too big to be unwieldy, but it ain't so small you can't read the words either. The gold tassel for marking pages broke off a while back, but I can still see the threads coming up out of the

binding where it used to be. Reminds me of how much use it's had. The pages got this red color on the edges, so when the book is closed it looks all red. All blood red. It's the blood, all right. It is that. The lettering is crisp and clear, easy to read. Nothing fancy, except maybe the gold text on the front but that's only to be expected. His Words are all marked out in red too. I quite like the feel of this book.

Long is getting his blood up for something, just looking for what. If he wasn't Mr. Day's son, he woulda been sent on his way a while back. It's too bad. For that little girl. She's a sweet one. If I had a daughter I woulda liked her to be like Molly. Maureen ain't a bad woman neither, but I gotta wonder about how she ever got messed up with Long in the first place.

Lord, grant me that I may use your Word through my tongue to get through to the people. I'll do the best I can, in my meager capacity to get it through. There is forgiveness in every human heart. This I do believe.

He's coming over here now, Rudy, that hangdog expression on his face, those scared little eyes set back a ways in his skull, shifting. He's rubbing his hands together as he does often. He got one of them conditions, with those tics. He's all ragged. Still, out there, rubbing down them statues... Lord, he's a stubborn one. He walks real slow, shuffling sort of, up to my table. He ain't quite looking at me with his little kid eyes in his old man head.

"Hey Rudy. You need something?" I say.

He ain't saying nothing. He's sort of looking past me, behind me at something, but there ain't nothing there. Gives folks the creeps. But I like having him around though. I honestly do.

God's charity knows no bounds and giving it to them who are a bit touched is the best you can do with it, I suppose.

"I said, you need something Rudy?" I say again.

This time he looks me in the eye. I've noticed many a time how quickly Rudy's eyes can change. He normally has that dazed, hangdog look on him. Sad eyes. Sometimes though, he flashes a bit of smarts under them, makes you think about what goes on in that old man head of his.

"Uh. Sorry to bother you, Sal, just wanted to know what all you like me to do this morning," he says.

He's shifting around a bit. Rubbing his hands. Breaks my heart. I cannot know what kind of suffering this man has endured and, Lord's truth, I don't want to. Maybe that's why he never speaks of it.

"We're gonna have sermon at ten. It's what, round eight now? I don't reckon there's much to be done before then. Take some time to yourself, if you want," I say.

He has some books and things in his bunk. Ain't much, but a man needs some time alone. I've seen him before, sitting on his little cot cause he leaves his door open at times, just sort of staring out. Thinking, I'd say, bout what though I would not dare to guess at. Can't send him outside to work in this wind though. As he said, it might rain in a bit and wouldn't make sense anyway.

"All right then. Thanks," he says.

He starts shuffling off towards the door. His shoes scraping along the linoleum.

I wonder if he's always been like this, or if something happened to him to make him this way. When I asked him to stay here, I probed as I could, as I felt proper, but didn't get nothing from him except that he was from Tennessee and did some odd jobs for his Pa after he finished high school. Either way, he's been like this for some time, I would imagine, and it can't make for an easy life.

"You can always read this," I say and show him my Bible.

'In his utmost extremity, a man can turn to the Lord and find his peace.' But normal folks can take actions to ease the unknowable pain of a fellow traveler. He shuffles on out and I can hear the wind blowing hard when he opens the door. When it closes the noise dies out and the dust settles down around the threshold, still and quiet.

And that Long staring at him the whole time like a hollow.

III

The nails driven deep in the naked flesh. The sun burning down, scalding, parching, relentless. Surely this is as it should be, for I have forsaken the covenant of man unto man and having thus broken the law, submit to my humiliation, torment and punishment. I steel myself and prepare to jettison the flesh.

He sits in the office among the books and brochures. He holds a bible, closed, in his right hand. Closed are his eyes and he rubs his closed eyes with his left hand. He rakes his fingers back through his thinning gray hair. He has mud on his shoes. The mud is caked and dry around the sides, but wet and leaving traces on the soles.

The office door opens.

The other thief with me, he screams. His hands clench and unclench wildly. His eyes all rage, all hatred. He curses the soldiers. His mouth a rotting hole. Broken and crooked teeth. His lips crack, white and dust laden. Fear behind his mask of fury.

Long enters the office. Don and Si follow behind and close the door again. The door is now closed. They look down at Rudy with conspiracy.

-Howdy there, Rudy, Long says.

Long sits down on the bench next to Rudy and lays his arm out behind him. The other two stand there, immobile and silent. Don looks on expectantly, the cracking calm of his face betraying a seething desire. His swollen belly sits heavy in his overalls. Si is empty, distant. He looks up at the ceiling.

-Hiya, Long, Rudy says.

If a man steals and that man loses his hand and justice is meted and that be done for infringement on the natural rights of men, property included, it warrants retribution of, if not equal to, then fitting the character of, and upon this stake of wood I am bared for my transgression of the laws of man and thus steel for the inevitable jettisoning of this flesh. They prepare to raise another. He writhes on the ground beneath me, as I have writhed, his confession etched above him as mine. The other thief beside me stares down at this newly arrived also, but with scorn. He tilts his head slowly toward mine, his eyes meet mine and he laughs with wild brutality.

-You know why they call me "Long," Long asks, grinning.

Rudy remains silent.

Long laughs.

-You know my name's Luke. That's what folks call me who ain't my friend, Long says.

-All right, Rudy says.

-Luke ain't such a bad guy, Long says. Why, he's a saint.

Don laughs.

-Working hard, then? Long asks.

-Sal said ain't nothing to do 'til after the sermon, Rudy says.

-Issat so? Well, did ya'll hear that? Ain't no work to do until after the sermon! Long says.

Don laughs and grunts. Si is silent, distant, but present and partial.

-That's real strange, Rudy. Sally told us we gotta clean up the grounds and keep on at Conroy's old truck 'til it runs, sermon or no. We gotta do it now. You reckon we can wait then, Rudy, if there ain't no work 'til after the sermon? Long says.

-I don't know, Long. Sal only told me what to do, Rudy says.

-Guess you must be special, Rudy. Sally must have a special place in his heart just for you. How about it? Are you special? Long says.

They raise this one up, in the middle, between me and the other thief. We both pivot our necks, with a crying out of strength, to see his face between us. I see his flesh, his hair, his sweat, his blood. I feel the violation of the metal through his body as it is in my own. I taste the arid lack in his mouth. I see across him, to the other, who cackles madly still, making crude insults to those below and watching with peculiar intensity, this one in the middle, newly risen.

-He told me I could read my bible, Rudy said.

-He said you could read your bible? That's mighty good, Rudy. How is that Bible? You get to any of the good parts yet? The ones where all them boys get their heads cut off and all the pretty girls get kidnapped and raped? Long asked.

Don laughs a deep, dark grunt. Si betrays an emotion on his face. He distances. Long smiles wide, his hand on Rudy's shoulder. Rudy looks away, towards the floor, and says nothing. Long leans in close and Rudy can smell his breath.

-You ever been with a girl, Rudy? Long asks.

The other thief and I read the sin of the one newly raised. But it is not a charge. It is a statement. It cannot be true. I do not understand. The other immediately laughs loud, coughing and spitting up blood. He says, "If that indictment is true, if you really are him, then why don't you save yourself – and us!" He laughs again and spits upon the ground, the dryness of the soil soaking up his life and dissipating it into nothing.

-I asked you a question, son. C'mon now. You're what, forty-five, fifty, I reckon. You a monk or something? You been laid,

Rudy, don't play around. I bet you been laid plenty. Old man like you. Shit. Or don't you like girls, Long says.

Rudy says nothing, does nothing. Long leers at Rudy and grips his shoulder tightly. Rudy submits to the squeezing, to the leering. Don laughs again, his big belly shaking slowly, his deep voice echoing in the empty room. Si just stands there, watching, not quite looking away, but restrained and aloof, his hands in his pockets. For a moment there is no movement in the room except Long's heavy breathing.

because if there is judgment then there is justice and there must be justice in order for us to go on for we cannot go on without order and there is no order without justice and there is no justice without judgment and who is to be the judge if not the men in the position to judge and condemn or set free? But this man with no crime on his head, is it justice, does he belong here on this hill with the endless rows of the dead hanging from the sky and dripping into the ground and disappearing and does the hot earth deserve to drink his blood with ours, commingling in the soil and bringing forth some nightmare fruit from the skull on which we are perched and the birds above circling for their share when the soldiers go away and they are the keepers of justice, but are men, and unjust, and how can there be order or justice or judgment by men who are above all disorderly, unjust and biased? Have I waited too long to separate from my flesh as the pain of the world burns into my lungs and wrists and I breathe in the death that will consume the little fire of my being and the other one there continues and continues his poison spitting over this man who has no crime on his head he has no crime to speak of and this cannot be justice for though I have stolen and am where I should be, who is this other to speak of the man in the middle with such arrogance? No, this cannot be right. This cannot be right. Then the man in the middle looks at me and his face becomes as sunfire, withering me to ashes.

Long throws a punch at Rudy's face and stops inches short. Rudy flinches terribly. Long and Don laugh hysterically. Si smiles a bit but only with his mouth.

-Hell, Rudy, we're just messing with you. You're a good old boy. You're like a little kid. A little brother I always wanted. Even if you are some kind of retard, Long says.

Long motions toward the door with his head. Si is out the door immediately. Don gives Rudy one last look, bares his teeth, and follows. Long goes to the door and has his hand on the knob when he turns back and stares at Rudy.

"Be quiet!" I say. "How can you mock a man sharing in your very own pain? Do you not fear? He shares our torment and not our crime," I say. My heart burns. It may explode. My lungs have little left. My muscles are slack and waning. I cannot see but the sky. The man in the middle looks towards me, annihilating me with his gaze. I say to him, "Remember me when you go to your kingdom."

-You stay the hell away from Molly, you hear me? And Maureen too. You creep me the hell out and I don't want to see you talking or even looking at my girls. You got it? I'm serious now, you hear, Long says.

He doesn't wait for Rudy to answer before leaving and slamming the door to the office behind him. Rudy stares at the floor, gripping his bible with shaking hands.

"Today," he replies, "you will be with me in paradise."

IV

still I was glad I got Molly that dress and had her wear it today
for the service even though he doesn't like me to do it with his
fear not being able to accept something as simple as this
without getting all ruffled feathers and making a big scene
about it at breakfast in front of everyone like every time any
little thing goes on he has to let everyone know he's in charge
all over again embarrassing himself and everyone else who has
to watch it like they aren't already used to the way he is the
way he sits there even now with that bored look on his face like
this is such a chore and he has better things to do than spend
Sunday morning in church with his family

things a man can't show in public feelings they aren't supposed
to feel but all of them do saving them up for the bedroom and
letting them out like a crack in a dam spilling all over us when
the lights get turned off and the warmth of our bodies wraps
them up in the covers and they begin to speak those secret
things that a woman might say out in the daylight but for a man
are reserved for only those private times which is why none of
them know really that he is a good man how could they know
who Luke even is without spending those times with him like I
have and hearing him talk in his quiet voice about those things
he won't admit to the rest of the world that knows him as Long
and that's how I know he's a good man no matter what they
might say and even if Sally stares over at him all day I'll know
that he's a good man and a good father and that deep down he
loves me and Molly and I know these things and I've heard them
spoken from rough lips in the dark when only the truth is light
enough to come out

"Thank you all for coming out this Sunday," Father Sal says from the podium. "Real good to see all your faces. Today I'd like to talk about what I consider to be a cornerstone of our faith and tradition: forgiveness."

Sally speaking directly to us to me to Luke trying to get through to us and yes I feel I feel the Lord but getting through to Luke making him understand and come around is going to take time but he will come around and he will understand Long who never forgave anyone long as I've known him man can keep a grudge but sometimes with men the blood gets to boiling and there's no stopping it until it explodes and smashes against something like a runaway train or a crack in the dam exploding and exploding until the pressure's all worked out and then they go right back to bottling it up again and we wait and wait and wait for the next time it gets to be too much and he's always saying how he didn't mean it and I know he didn't mean it when he speaks to me in his quiet voice afterwards and the way he caresses me so gentle and tells me what a sorry son of a bitch he is and gets that look like a puppy that just don't know any better looking at you again and again never meaning it but bottling and bottling and can't help but blow over at times it's the way of men hiding in the daylight

"-without sin cast the first stone.' I ask you, fine ladies and gentlemen, who here could throw that stone?"

but he is a good father there's that and he might be overprotective the way fathers are but he loves her as I do and wouldn't hurt her he promised me that one time when he come back all hangdog he promised me it wouldn't ever happen and he's been good to his word because I know him deep down the way these others never could the way only a woman can know a man and anyway he's working on it for me too he promised that the last time he's working on it and he'll find a way he promised after all, he is a good father there's that and Molly's such a good girl and so sweet she's been raised right and I have to give him credit for that a lot of men can't father can't even abide children and Lord knows Luke ain't perfect but she is going to grow up to be a good woman and I have to give him credit for that I have to give him that

"-men find the Lord not through purity, but through defilement. Men come to the light out of the darkness. Men have their sins washed away not because they are already clean, but because they are dirty,"

Sally looking over here real intent like he has a point looking at Luke looking down on him like all his words are just for him like he's just the personal mouthpiece for the Lord come to speak right at Long to make him change his ways like it's just that simple like you can just speak words to a man and hope for him to change like you can just skip over all the nights and feelings a woman puts in to help her man like he's just going to see the light and change and Sal not even knowing him not even seeing Luke as Luke but more as Long more as that Long and the boys and not even liking him much the way most don't on account of how he seems and I know he has a way with people and I guess if that's all they know about him I can't blame them much but that's because a man is an iceberg and you only see that little part he intends to show unless you put in the years, night after night, raise their blood and listen to their quiet voice

"-you might want to think about it for a second. Think about that beam in your eye first. We got so much lumber we could build another church! But no matter how big our beam is, it's always easy to see right past it and into the speck of another,"

comin out to his Daddy's place like this asking him for work and doing things here and there that he wouldn't get paid for anywhere else but by family and saying that he can provide for us and that it won't be long fore we pick up and go somewhere else but it's been a long long time

that poor Rudy standing alone in the back there by himself looking down like he's listening but who knows if he can hear or grasp any of this and no I can't abide the way Long treats him it ain't right I know that I know it I know Long oughta leave him alone and I can see why Sally gets upset about it that Rudy ain't much different from Molly when it comes down to it man barely speaks keeps to himself barely leaves the grounds he's an older man now but he's still someone's son and some mother at some time felt about him how Luke feels about Molly but Long can't see things that way not yet and why him and those other boys go about picking on him I just don't know I don't know what makes men do the things they do acting crazy at every occasion writing cruelties into the fabric of their experience where a woman can see the mother's child through to the present

except that Sally the way he treats Rudy took a shine to him right off like as pastor he's mother and father but that Rudy that Rudy someone really has to do something someone really has to someone should really do something

the way it is with me and Luke we sort of have to balance out like Molly's dress how I bought it and how I'll buy her another one and how he got down on her for it and how he'll get down on me for spending the money but I just have to keep him balanced out until he gets himself together and figures it all out because deep down I know he loves me I've seen him in the quiet in the dark felt his heartbeat and his touch which can be gentle so gentle like none would ever believe of the man they think they know though I've heard his soul speak to me in a whisper I could lose in the wind and I know God will forgive him and I pray to the Blessed Virgin he will come round and I know he will show them all how he can be the good man he is down deep where down deep he is a good man where down deep he does love me where down deep he does love Molly too where down deep he does the best he can the best he can the best he can

V

We need to fix a new axle on it. That's all there is to it. I already told them that. We spent all that time trying to fix the one that's on it now. But it's all rusted out. Everybody knows it. Can't be no good no more. Not when it's all eat away like that. Where Doc Conroy got that truck, I don't know. We been working on fixing it now for a while. The engine was near shot. Would have been faster to just replace it. Maybe cheaper too. I told them that at the time. Now we need that new axle. The man could afford a new truck anyway.

"Think about the beam in your eye first. We got so much lumber we could build another church!"

That would be nice work. Working on cars is good. Working with wood is better, I figure. I like it more. I built that barn addition with my dad that summer. Last time I cut wood. Wood don't speak. Metal don't speak. Makes easy work. I hope James got that work for me up in Amarillo. I could want more to build some houses now than work on that old junker another day in this damn heat. That Conroy, rather have us bustin' our balls fixing that jalopy than buy hisself a new truck that he could buy no problem. Amarillo's lookin' real good.

"...one stray sheep. One sinner repenting. The greater the sin, the more befouled the sinner, the greater the glory in his redemption..."

Why Long gotta run up that old boy every chance he gets, I just don't know. He is a weird dude, Rudy. No doubt about that. But it don't mean he needs to be treated so rough, the way Long does it. I would say something but Long's my friend and all. Better not to get in the middle. Long's real good with the tools. He does a good job, usually. When he isn't on the drink. I mean we drank a few beers when we worked outside, me and James, but not the hard stuff and not that much. But Long does good work, mostly. Like how he did with that gearbox that was all tore up. Work with him day in and day out. Wouldn't stand to have some trouble between us, working in such close corners. I'd rather just spend my time working on cars and trucks and the like. Building something when it needs building. Hands on the metal. Hands on the wood. Without much speaking at all.

"...which is easier, to say 'your sins are forgiven' or to entreat a crippled man to stand up and walk?"

Rudy reminds me of Clint. I ain't never talked to Rudy none. So it might not be the same thing. If they can even figure out what that sort of thing is. I don't think there's any knowing the way people are. Especially if they ain't right. I wouldn't wanna be in his shoes. Not Clint's neither. Always felt bad about feeling that, but it's true all the same, Lord help me. It's no kind of world to be less than a man. But what could I do?

Don still got my torque wrench. I'll have to ask him about that after the service. I like that one quite a bit. It has a no-slip grip. It cranks real good. The fit for the bits is tight. It's well made. But I reckon if I get that work in the city I won't much need it. I'll give it to Don anyway, most likely. I could take or leave Don, to be honest, but I wouldn't want to be on his bad side.

But I spent plenty of time around my brothers. Me and James and Clint, toolin' around. Joined at the hip growing up. Before they sent Clint away. There wasn't nothing wrong with him. I mean, he wasn't bad or anything. He just had a way of not being able to show or tell anyone how or where he was. He had that empty look, same as Rudy. Just sort of sat there. Looking at you like you weren't there. He wasn't no good on the farm. Or with tools. His hands were slow. His body moved like it struggled with how he told it to do. He the one first called me Si. Hey Si, he said. Hey. If things go too far with Rudy, I reckon I'll step in. It's mostly Long teasing.

"..because 'he who has been forgiven little, loves little.' A man cannot love unless he has first wronged and then repented..."

I'd rather just work on the truck. If we never get it to run right I'll be okay with just working to make it so, day in and day out. Long is my friend anyway. With his wife and little girl running around, he's cautious about people. Says Rudy creeps him out. Says, 'Si, if you were in my shoes, you'd know why.' If he's half on the nose with all he talks. Caution ain't a bad idea. But sometimes he gets downright cruel. I would step in. I figure I would. But trouble's trouble. I wonder if James would let me stay at his place. He's got that extra bedroom. That Laura don't like me much, but we're brothers and James gotta let me stay, at least for a little while. We're brothers after all.

VI

Oh and here comes Father Sal. Sal, Father Sal! That was a lovely sermon. It really spoke to me. I think the Word got out today.

Thank you, Bernice, he says. Always nice to hear. He's a very kind man, if a little short with you after his sermons. But everyone always pulls at him from all sides and you can't expect him to give you his attention for too long.

Maureen's waiting on him, got an armful of folders for him. It's always business with her. I know it's her job, but really, with a little girl like that and married to, to, to that man... she ought focus more on family. That's what I did at her age and my sons are growed and have their own families now.

Oh and there's Rudy, standing hunched over, rubbing his hands, looking at Sal like he's gonna say something, but everyone's pushing him out of the way to crowd Sal and shake his hand. I never had a problem with Rudy myself, mind you, but the way I hear it, is that he ain't put together right. You know the type. He seems nice enough but most of them do, until they don't, if you take my meaning. He's harmless enough, I suppose. He sure takes his share from Long and the other boys though. That's the way of things. When my boys were young they fought and fought. Meanness in them, 'til it isn't. My Ed, rest his soul, would have called Rudy a stub.

Look at him, just standing there, staring up into the sky like a statue. Why nothing's up there but a rain cloud, boy. Well, someone might as well do something.

Rudy, I say, you all right? He looks at me like I woke him up and he smiles at me, nice enough, but a little off, and says Yes, Ms. Bernice, I okay, just thinkin' it gonna rain. That's a fact, I say and look up with him. The cross is way up there, standing tall and proud like the Lord himself, protecting all us down here. You can feel God's own power coming down like off the mountain. Lord almighty, yes. But he's just staring up at it, not saying anything, shuffling and fidgeting. Sal calls them his tics. You're best not to acknowledge them, I suppose, but they are a bit distracting.

Rudy, why don't you come by the den tonight and we'll play some cards, I say. He doesn't say anything, just keeps staring up there so I say it again. Times you have to tell him twice for him to hear. He looks at me this time, like a lost child, then smiles and says, Yes ma'am, that sound nice. Do you think you have some of them cookies? Well, I had to get another box the last time he came over. Yes Rudy, I have some. You don't eat too many though okay, I say. He nods and looks up again.

I need to talk to Maureen about taking a few days; she can be a stickler for the paperwork, even if she's a nice person. You want some time off you better let her know. I take the same time every year, it was my and Ed's anniversary. I told her before it would be the same time. She says you can't apply for vacation more than six months in advance.

She's still talking to Sal so I lean back against the wall and wait, watching that little girl of hers run around, twirling and jumping. She is a darling; you ain't seen none cuter or more full of life. Ed was always glad we never had a daughter, but if he saw this one running around like she does he might have changed his mind.

She goes over to where Rudy is, still looking up at the sky and she says Rudy, whatcha lookin at and he doesn't say anything, just keeps staring up and she says again Rudy, Rudy, I said whatcha doin, whatcha lookin at? He doesn't look down at her, but he says I just lookin up at the cross, Ms. Molly. Thinkin bout how big it is and how it must look from up in them clouds. Thinkin bout how the farther up you go, the smaller and smaller this cross would look, til you couldn't even see it at all, he says. You oughtn't say such things to a child. Molly looks up, puzzling out words she probably doesn't even know and then says You sound awfully sad. Whatsa matter? Rudy finally looks at her with his odd, stone face and says I all right. Just the weather. You run along now, go find your mama and see if she need any help.

Good advice. He ain't so bad or as dumb as people reckon. Most people aren't, you know. Molly starts pointing over here and says She's right over there. We're goin back into town today, to the shops! I love the shops, don't you? He scrunches up his brow and says I don't go too often. Ain't got much money and there ain't nothin there for an old man anyways. But you all have a good time, okay. See if you can get some ice cream. Ice cream real good. He's rubbing his hands real fast now, shuffling his feet, looking away and up. Sometimes they get nervous around young ones. I've seen it before.

Maureen, finished up with Sal, calls out Molly, Molly! and the girl comes running over, tugging Rudy's sleeve along with her, pulling him over to stand right next to me. Sal is still flipping through the folders Maureen gave him so I just wait where I am, watching him and listening to Molly clamor on, only cause I'm standing right here of course. I'm no snoop.

Mama, Mama, she says, can old Rudy come with us to town? He sounds sad and needs the company, she says. Rudy makes to protest but she just goes on, tugging his sleeve and swinging his arm back and forth. So can he, Mama, can he? Maureen puts her arm around Molly and guides her arm off of Rudy's sleeve. Hi Rudy, she says, you all right? He wipes his face. He's sweating a bit, can't blame him. It's rather hot, considering the rainstorm that's coming, but he can't get it all, like his hands don't know how to work his face. Ed, bless him, always said you should feel Jesus through kind works. I suppose I'll just have to help this stub out a little bit. Sometimes you got to.

They finish talking and Molly runs off, dances off more like, happy, so I guess they convinced him to go with them out into town. I say Rudy, ya'll goin into town with Maureen? and he says Yes Ma'am, Ms. Bernice, I suppose. Ain't for goin into town much, but Ms. Molly and Ms. Maureen want it. He's shifting from leg to leg, restless, and rubbing his hands together like you've never seen.

I say Well all right then, but come over here first, you're sweaty as a pig and won't do to go into town looking like a ranch hand. You leave that to them other boys. So I take his handkerchief and dab his face a bit, drying it off and he's staring at the floor with his sad little eyes and making tiny circles in the dust with his foot. I dab him off and hand it back to him and say You all take care in town now. We'll raincheck that card game, you hear. I'll keep the cookies in supply.

He nods and shuffles off, looking up at the top of the cross. Dark clouds up there now, rain won't be long, you can tell when you've seen enough storms. But Lord, I wish Ed was here to see this with me because he loved God and Jesus with his whole heart and I know he'd approve of any kindness to a stub like Rudy. I think he looks down on me from up there, you see. He watches over me in the bosom of the Lord and will take me into his arms when it's my time to finally join him.

I guess I'll talk to Maureen after she gets back, because I'm taking those days off one way or another. You can bet on that.

VII

Just look at the desolation here, Rudy. Half of these shops are empty and the other half might as well be. This town is finished. Dried up. Dead. It's quiet out. IT IS SO QUIET. That's right, rub your little hands, Rudy, rub, rub, rub. The way the dust blows across the sidewalk. DOESN'T IT REMIND YOU OF SOMETHING? Look at yourself in the rearview. Just take a look. LOOK AT YOURSELF.

They pull up into a parking space outside Chick's Clothing Store. Maureen guides the pickup between the lines and sets it in park. Molly beams and looks anxiously at Rudy who clumsily opens the door lock, undoes his seatbelt and opens the door. He carefully steps out of the truck, feeling some pain in his left knee, and then helps Molly down out of the cab. Maureen gets out on the other side. He closes the door behind them.

LOOK

Stop trying to pretend. You're in it just like everyone else. Buried in the shit and the piss and the filth. Crawling through it, writhing in it, empty inside and tearing at anything you can reach. Trapped inside. In the Earth just like just like JUST LIKE trapped inside. Hahahaha. She twirls and dances. She moves across the rotting wood patio. She can't escape it, Rudy. You know that. SHE IS IN IT. She WILL BE. You can no more be other than you can stop. I'll tell you. I'll tell you about that dry pain, that slow burn, the drinking of sand in an hour of fire and borne and buried into your breast forever. I WILL TELL YOU HOW IT BURNED.

-Well, come on Rudy, Maureen says, holding Molly on the shoulders.

-I gonna just set out here a bit, if ya'll don't mind. Take your time though, I gonna park it on this bench and watch the town a while, take in some town air, Rudy says, looking out into the empty street.

-All right. We'll only be a bit. Molly's gonna try on this dress and then we'll be ready, Maureen says.

-Take your time. Take as long as you need, Rudy says.

Molly and Maureen enter the store. Rudy sits down on a swinging wooden bench and looks at the shops across the street.

Antique store. Do you remember the antique store you worked at? Do you remember the old man and the old woman who ran it? Remember they had that little porcelain lamb that was all white, unpainted? Little white lamb. Little white lamb. You didn't buy it. You drank of the sand, acolyte of the sand, buried in the sand, in your mouth, eyes and ears, buried alive BURIED ALIVE in the sand and burning, eternal, into the hollow.

Don't get so upset. When I burned upon the skull I saw many a man deceiving himself out of pain. Not just you. With the metal in the flesh and the skin torn by wood and the sun blazing down

141 | the largest cross

and the burning in the chest, there is no escape. Not for kings or false kings, not for thieves and not for any sinning creature, suffering his time upon the Earth. You can't escape this. YOU ARE IN IT. Even the king dies upon the cross.

Rudy thinks about going into town, shopping, with a woman and a little girl. He had never done that before. He had never been married. He had never had children. He was out shopping on Main Street on a Sunday after church. It's what folks do.

You just wanted to feel good. You just wanted to do good. He wanted good too. But he writhed and cried like any helpless man. His only kingdom was death, the kingdom with many kings. Everyone sits on the throne. And I saw the fear in his eyes as his soul left his body. I saw it in his face. IN THE BURNING there is naught but fear and in life there is naught but suffering and only fools pretend to more.

The door to the shop opens. Molly comes running out, her little shoes clacking against the wooden porch.

-Rudy, look at this dress! Isn't it magnificent? Molly says, twirling around in front of him.

The bottom of the dress lifts up as she twirls and twirls around with her. She twirls around and around. She finally stops and looks up at him with her laughing little angel face.

-Well, ain't it pretty? Ain't it the prettiest dress you ever seen? she says.

-It beautiful. You beautiful, Ms. Molly.

YOU CANNOT CHANGE the world. It is a gauntlet of pain and desire, crushing hopes and bodies with relentless scorn and you know that misery reigns, you know that the heart of man is black and rotting, that the heart seeks its own temptation, that all is possible, all acceptable, that everything breaks down in the face of desire that NOTHING CHANGES. Men are monsters and monsters are real and even the king dies afraid.

Rudy's hands tremble.

-Your daddy gonna like it, I bet, he says.

-You think so? Thanks, Rudy! I like it a lot too. It is beautiful, ain't it? Molly says.

Embers hurled against the darkness. Desperate clawing against the tidal dune. Swallow whole the earth of men and digest its sand in gluttonous derision. Cracked keystones of falling arches and cities decimated with the wasting disease and into the blue of night rush the murderers to some hapless prey, themselves unaware, flailing to the indolent and arbitrary rotation of the fixed stars above. Hahaha.

Molly twirls again and leaps into the air, dancing her finest. She gives Rudy one last laughing glance and runs back into the store.

There is a festering wound in the corpse of the man, eaten out by maggots, green and black with decay, eating away, eating away and distending and the features are vague on the face pulled over the skull and the eyes say nothing and are the first devoured and behind their windows is only blackness and I have seen the king in his purple procession mount the skull and take his wooden throne and I have seen the king speak to his subjects of joining him in his kingdom and I have seen the blood run down his face and into the dust and I have seen the king's burning death and tasted his fear at the moment of reunion. You know what you are. Now and ever. Unto the assimilation, unto the void.

The king is dead in burning death. Long live the king in burning life.

VIII

I got a vanilla with cherries. Mama got a lemon sore bay. Old Rudy got a vanilla cone. The ice cream is real good. I like coming to town. In town they have clothes and ice cream and all kinds of doodads and toys. I wonder if Rudy likes his ice cream. I sure like mine.

"Is your ice cream good, Rudy?" I say.

"Yess'm, it real good, for sure. How bout yours?" he says with a mouthful of ice cream. You ain't supposed to talk when you got food in your mouth, but I guess Rudy can get away with it, being touched and all, like Mama says. Mama's barely eating hers, but she's always like that. Maybe she doesn't like ice cream as much as me and Rudy. I hope I never stop liking it.

Mama usually buys me ice cream but this time Rudy bought it for me and Mama. That's real nice of him. Daddy bought us ice cream one time, last summer and it was real nice. I liked it when Daddy came out here. But he's real busy workin' for grampa. One time he let me sit in Doc's truck.

"Now, aren't you glad you came out with us, Rudy?" Mama says. "You need to get out every once in a blue moon. It does you some good."

"Yeah, ain't you glad?" I say. Mama's right. It's good for Rudy to come with us. Mama says people need to be around people or they get sad. I like living at the cross cause there's always people there. Not many other kids though.

Rudy nods, still munching on his ice cream cone. He might like ice cream even more than me. He's been staring at his ice cream since he got it, not even looking up to talk to us.

"You know," Mama says, "we don't really know a whole lot about you, Rudy. You been workin' at the cross since Luke and me showed up but we never really talked. You got family in Texas or something?"

Rudy stops eating his ice cream but keeps on looking at it like it's gonna talk to him or something. But he's smiling a little, so he must be happy.

"No ma'am, I ain't had no family since I live with my Pa back in Tennessee." Rudy says. "That a ways back. Stayed at home for a while after high school when I couldn't find no work, then I pick up and move. Ain't never been married or had no kids. On the road for a while, maybe ten years back, I reckon, then I come here and meet Father Sal and I working for him ever since. Don't mind it though. Father Sal real nice and I like working there. I do all right."

How come he never had no kids? Rudy's older than Daddy by a lot and he ain't had no kids or been married or nothing? I'm gonna get married as soon as I can and have lots of kids.

"Family's a great thing," Mama says, "There are ups and downs to be sure. Even in the best situations, it can be tough sometimes. Lord knows Luke and me don't always see eye to eye." Mama laughs and looks out the window a bit like she saw something out there.

"But we work it out, you know? And kids, kids are great. Molly here is the best thing that ever happened in my life. She's my pride and joy," Mama says.

Mama's talkin' about me. I'm gonna have my own pride and joys one day. I hope Rudy does too. I bet Rudy would be a good daddy.

"My family didn't ever much work like that," Rudy says.

IX

Rudy sat in his room back at the cross. He sat on the edge of his bed, quiet, looking into the small mirror above the dresser. He ran his hand through his thinning hair and across his bald spot. He wiped the rain off his face. He shivered. He looked into the mirror and tried to recognize the face that stared back at him.

Knees in the dust, pushed down by overbearing weight. This burden, this burden, O Father, I crumple beneath it like a leaf. I can see the hill, the path, the crosses coming up into the skyline. I feel it in me, ready to burst and You repeat that I must endure. If this is me, if this is for me, if this is what it must take, Thy will be done.

In the mirror was the person people talked to during the day. This old, gentle, timid man. When Molly laughed. When Maureen was kind. When Long was cruel. When Sal was compassionate. When Conroy was indifferent. When Ms. Bernice played cards. This person, this face, bore them all and reflected back to them what they expected to see.

For I have lived my life not by any written tenet, but by the law of my heart, inscribed by my Father, needing no interpretation from priests, requiring no tithe or donation, but only kindness, love, and truth. For I have discarded the laws of my people and torn the garments of their leaders. For I have felt in my own self the guilt of men and the weight of their contrition, bottled inside their souls like roaming ghosts, haunting their flesh until it withers away and they may be free. For I have taken it upon myself to die in their name, sharing in their guilt and burden with the compassionate love available to all people.

The man with this face could be married. He could have a family. This man could have children and go into town with his own family. He could go shopping for his little girl and buy her a dress. He could buy her ice cream. The man with this face could do anything at all. He could remain silent. He could be an idiot. He could let them assume about him and accept their condescension.

I have fallen and there are none about to assist me. These final moments I must spend alone and shoulder what hardships may come, alone. I take up my cross and walk into the field of my own death. My ghost trembles. Father, I approach.

Rudy smiled. He watched himself smile in the mirror. This kind of smile made people smile back. He thought of Molly twirling in her new dress.

Just spinning around and around and around.
Just spinning.
He pictured her spinning.
Around and around.

Twirling around in her new dress. Ain't it the prettiest. Ain't it.
Twirling around. Spinning around.
Around and around.
Around and around and around.

X

Hahahaha.
Now this should be good.
Look at him, standing there. Walking out into the slaughter.
Dumb fuck.

Hahaha. I'm gonna enjoy the shit out of this. I nudge Si. He
don't look too thrilled. I wonder about him.

Long gonna whoop him good. Break him. Finally give the old
retard what he's been asking for. Like a cripple deer in the
forest.

-Howdy, Rudy. Long says. He's drunk. That's all right. I'll clean
up for him if he can't. I been waiting to get my hands on
someone.

Rudy don't say nothing, course. He knows what's coming. Even
a fuckup like him can smell this kind of trouble. He's shaking and
rubbing his goddamn hands together. He's scared. Hell, he's
always scared. Put him out of his misery already.

-So, Maureen says ya'll had a great time in town today. Went
and did some shopping? Went and had a little ice cream? Long
says.

-Do you like ice cream? I say.

-That sounds like a real good time, Rudy. Did you enjoy it? Long says. Long walks up to him now, standing face to face.

I feel the blood in my hands. I'm ready. I'm tired of this waiting. Long wants to toy with him but I'm ready to start the real fun. I wanna watch him bleed. Rudy still ain't saying shit. Standing there like a statue, that stupid expression on his face. Doesn't he know how it all works. It's all so simple. So simple.

-He asked you a question, boy! I say. He jumps a little bit. Hahaha.

-Don's right. I asked you if you had a good time. Did you or didn't you go into town with my wife and my daughter? Long says. My head is pounding. It's time to get this out. It's been too long.

-I did, Long. We had a good time. Rudy says.

Now he's done it. That's about it. That's gonna do it. It's almost time. Long turning all red, grabbing Rudy's collar and pulling him in close.

-WHO THE FUCK DO YOU THINK YOU ARE, WEIRDO? Long says, screaming into his face. JUST WHO IN THE FUCK? Didn't I tell you to stay the hell away from them? Just this morning? You goddamn retard. Creeping around into other people's business. Did you think I was joking or that I wouldn't know?

Long's shaking him real good. He got his arms at his sides like a rag doll. He ain't gonna fight back or even defend himself. That's fine by me. Hahaha. I might even like it better. Just lay back and take what I got to give. That's the way Don does it.

-You told me. I didn't think you joking. I knew you know. Rudy says.

Long stops for a minute and I can tell this is it. It's just about here. Time to teach this boy a lesson. Time for him to learn it. Hahaha. Time to break his bones. Time to spill his blood. Hahahaha. Can't he see how simple it is?

I can feel it coming up. Long ready to burst. And the fear in that old boy's face like a tremor. I can smell it. I can see right through into his coward's heart. And it's about time to rip it right out of his chest. Haha.

Long cocks back his fist and I can feel my own blood hammering in my head. Such a rush. Hahaha. Now crush this little cockroach. Show him the way of the world. Haha.

Crush him.

Hahahahaha. Hahahaha.
Hahaha.

XI

Now I have to hit him.

So I do. So I hit him right in his face. Hard as I can. He crumples like a little doll. Like paper mache.

I'M TIRED OF YOU.
I'M TIRED OF SEEING YOU AROUND HERE.
WEIRDO.

He's spitting up blood now, getting on his hands and knees right where he belongs. None of them see it. Nobody else sees it, but

I know there's something wicked in him. I kick him as hard as I can in the ribs and I know how that feels and it takes the wind from him and he rolls on his back. Never felt so in the right.

YOU'RE HISTORY.
I WANT YOU GONE, UNDERSTAND? GONE.
I DON'T WANT TO SEE YOUR FACE AROUND HERE NO MORE.

He's lying on his back, blinking his eyes real quick like. Rain's washing away some of the blood coming out of his mouth. He's covered in mud. It's what he had coming. Stupid, old fool. To hell with him and all the rest of them anyway.

TO HELL WITH YOU.
RIGHT TO HELL WITH YOU.
AND WITH ANYONE ELSE.
HAND ME THAT BOTTLE, DON.

The wet bottle in my hand. I tilt it back, empty it, then smash it down on a rock right next to his stupid, lying head. The glass explodes and blood starts dripping from the cuts in his face. I'm burning. It's in me like the fire. Down my throat and into my chest and down and around, swirling, burning, and I could take this man's life right now and something inside me says to do it to snuff him out right here on his knees in the mud like a dog. But they're all watching. Don and Si are okay. That Doc Conroy. Not going to do nothing, like usual. Maureen. She best stay inside if she knows what's good.

YOU GET GONE AND STAY GONE.

A door opens. Sally. Fuck. Musta heard the bottle smash. Once he sees what's up it'll be over. I should kill him. I should kill this old man right now. It almost ain't even me saying it no more.

It's in me, more than me, pressing on me to do it now. There's something in the earth that wants to drink up his black blood. Sally's running. DO IT. DO IT NOW. DO IT NOW.

But Sal's already here.

-What in the hell is wrong with you, boy? he says to me.

NOTHING WRONG WITH ME, SALLY.
BUT THERE'S SURE AS SHIT SOMETHING WRONG WITH HIM.
I'M TELLING YOU.

-You're drunk, Long. You're drunk and you beat on this poor man. Look at him. How could you do this? How could you say these things? He's a gentle man, a simple man. You're a brute and a coward. He couldn't even defend himself, Long! What... why...

And it's like I can see what he's saying, but at the same time that ain't it at all. Sally never liked me anyway and I don't give two fucks about that, but he always been biased against me for no reason, or maybe cause my daddy's his boss, or maybe just cause he thinks I'm a degenerate, but he can't see what's right in front of his face with this shifty fool.

IT AIN'T LIKE THAT SALLY.

Then Maureen come up at me, hitting me on the chest and face, screamin at me.

-How could you? How could you? You animal! You evil bastard!

GO ON NOW.
GET BACK INSIDE.

THIS AIN'T ABOUT YOU.

GET BACK IN THE HOUSE NOW.

She moves toward him. To comfort him. The hell.

I SAID NOW.

She hesitates and then turns around and runs back to the house, cryin. I can still hear it calling me from down inside me. Like a man in my stomach hollering up through my own mouth to step on the neck while it's down and crush the windpipe. DO IT. But when Maureen gets to the house and opens the door, out runs Molly, out in the rain, white socks in the mud, crying and crying and crying and the fire leaves me altogether at once and I look down and see this Rudy slowly rollin back and forth on his side, breathin hard.

-Molly! Maureen calls.

But Molly just keeps runnin. I aim to catch her, but she loses her footing and slips in the mud. I start over to her, but she stands right back up, okay, and keeps coming on, covered in mud and somehow slips out of my hand and runs over to Rudy, leaning over him.

Her face is all muddy and wet with rain and tears. Her hair all matted against her head. Then I see the blood. She got blood on her arm and her knees where the bottle glass cut her.

Rudy looks up at her, first time he's moved since I knocked him down. He's starin at her and she's crying over him and he's staring, wild eyed, white as a sheet.

XII

pretty pretty
it just happened
never no good with woodwork
couldn't never level it
couldn't make it right

she so pretty
so small
so light
just wanted it to feel good

never meant for it to
hurt

she smiled at me
walkin home from somewhere
getting dark out and the trees rustlin in the wind
the mulch and needles kickin up under my feet
shufflin back home from the antique store

All I wanted was a little white lamb.

so pretty
she smiled at me and the buzzing seemed a bit better
I remember it got a little quieter

LOSER
RETARD
FUCKUP
CAN'T EVEN GET A GIRL
TWENTY YEARS OLD

stop it stop it stop it stop it stop it stop it stop it stop stop stop
im sorry daddy
im so sorry daddy

and she smiled at me and I smiled back at her
she didn't think I was so ugly
and she
so small and light
and I wanted to kiss her and she
WANTED
to kiss me back and she was
SHE STARTED SCREAMING
but I wanted to feel good
I wanted it to feel good
I wanted her to feel good
and the buzzing was so loud

my teeth scraping together
fit to burst inside my mouth
and I tell her no no no no no
it's gonna be fine
and she tellin me no no no no no
DOESN'T IT FEEL GOOD
and no no no
don't it
no no
then it
I never meant
but she
small
pretty
then she hardly moving
hardly talkin no more

and I knew what'd happened
she breathing strange
gasping
a goldfish on the floor
with some
blood
around her little round mouth
round little round little round mouth
so I pull her off into the trees
put her out of the way so no one wouldn't see her
tried to protect her

went home
didn't no one know
couldn't no one know
I made it up best I could but
never no good with woodwork

so it ain't square or level or what they say
and all the bugs and things
it wouldn't keep em out
they'd get her
blood, silence

and I told her im sorry im sorry im sorry
I wish I coulda built it better
but I never no good with my hands
im real sorry
this bad trouble real bad
so I put her in it
and put in my pillow and blanket
and told her I was sorry
and I knew

when I dig up the dirt out there in the trees
all the bugs and what have you
I tried to keep em away
the wind so loud
I tried
I didn't want to leave her there
but
but
so afraid
and I covering her up
hearin her rasp still
chokin like, gurgling
then
hearin it come from inside

scratch, scratch
scratch scratch scratch
scratch scratch scratch

and I cover my ears
sorry I couldn't build it better

scratch scratch
scratch

couldn't tell if it
things trying to get out
or
things trying to get in

got my hands over my ears
layin on the dirt, screamin
just screamin

but I still heard it
scratchin

and I knew they were
getting her

XIII

For anyone long engaged in the practice of observing human behavior, that which the majority of people most take for granted seems very strange and that which seems strange makes absolute sense.

For instance, observing a possibly handicapped older man beaten mercilessly in the street by an alcoholic, young never-do-well might encourage other people to actively intervene on his behalf. However, it is this very passion that incites these types of scenes to begin with. Intervene, do not intervene... All beginnings reach their conclusions regardless. The brief but bright explosions of violent emotion can never ultimately stand against the eternal inertia of matter, nor against the Unmovable Mover, nor against His transcendent light.

For one who does observe without active intervention does not derive pleasure from the viewing. Observation, in the strictest sense, is not voyeurism, nor the proverbial train wreck, but only a tragicomic banality with no impact on anyone or anything excepting the few fevered souls directly involved.

Father Salvatore hurries out to intervene. He is that type of man. When he arrived at the cross, I sought to ascertain his theological leanings and learned only that he carries a mace along with his bible and often prefers to wield it rather than the book. This is not judgment. Men of action co-exist beside men of contemplation, the obverse of their coin, and in the final analysis, equilibrium is achieved. This is why a contemplative man need not step in. A man of action, that hurried blood, will always be drawn to the erupting constellations of vigorous passion.

One cannot be considered enlightened or educated if one moves through the narrative of one's life without questioning one's own motivations and asking one's self difficult questions and giving one's self honest answers. The true contemplative does not envy the active. To clarify, the contemplative does not wish to be active, but does recognize the substantial lack of validation he receives from the many who take the active man upon their shoulders so readily after any brave, yet ill-conceived act. What they must know, subconsciously, yet refuse to admit into the milieu of their value system, is that for every man who runs into a burning building, there is a man, alone in a room with a book, using his God-given faculties to prevent the fire in the first place.

Now the girl has run out. Mr. Day said that he preferred to have his granddaughter live with him, out here in this arid compound. He loves children. He said that no divine revelation is possible without the continued presence of true innocents. But does he consider the happiness of the child, bereft of peers, in a difficult parental situation? He is a good man, and deserving of love. But he is an eccentric and his opaque reasoning often calls his decisions into question.

"Hello Doc," says a quiet, deep voice beside me. It is Mr. Day. This often happens, one thinks of him and he appears, though he is no devil.

I return his greeting with befitting cordiality.

"What happened here?" he asks calmly, almost rhetorically.

I inform him that his son, Luke, has put a beating on Rudolph.
The details are unnecessary. Mr. Day is a big picture person. He
nods as if he was just told that it is raining outside, but his face
betrays such a wealth of compassion that one immediately
forgives his apparent dismissal. Like many successful men, with
whatever criteria one uses to judge success, Mr. Day has a face
of great complexity. Each wrinkle earned through observation,
reflection, empathy, concern, hard decision, and perhaps even
misstep. He clasps me on the back with a friendly warmth.

"Please," he says.

I clear my throat, certainly barely audible above the rain, but
with enough gusto that it captures everyone's attention. Luke
stops in his tracks and looks up at his father with an instant
humility. Salvatore, who was attending to Rudolph, gives up his
gaze as well, still cradling the poor man in his arms. Maureen,
who ran out to restrain Molly, looks up as well and the tension
in her neck relaxes. Molly does not look up, still holding
Rudolph's hand and whispering softly in his ear. Rudolph too
does not acknowledge the presence, though he may have
slipped from consciousness. The situation has resolved itself.

Mr. Day looks out over them as the rain ceases. Could one
entirely decipher the lines of the human face, would one be
capable of withstanding their import? Many times I have asked
myself if Mr. Day is a man of action or a man of contemplation. I
have not decided.

What repercussions await those involved will come in their time and all things will continue on as before. There is shame in the faces of those who look up as their reason finally grasps their passionate excess of energy. Luke reluctantly goes for a talk with his father. Salvatore continues to look after Rudolph, who seems to be coming around. Maureen has taken Molly inside. Don and Simon have fled back into the shadows to soak in their secret remorse, if they still possess even that. Everything returns to its place.

XIV

A star explodes. Light races out in a sphere whose circumference is nowhere and whose center is everywhere.

XV

Stinging on my cheek. It sting. On my arm too. In my gut.
Got all clean up last night. Hunch over the toilet.
Hunch over the toilet, vomiting.
Father Sal pat me on the back and say "It's all right. It's all right."
Cause of he seen Long kick me in the gut.

Didn't want me on my chores today. Didn't want me out in the wind. It all muddy now and wet. The rain wash all the dirt off them statues, the one thief, the other one, and Jesus.

Look in the mirror again. I look in it. Back there, looking out, a broken old man.
That what I heard Ms. Maureen say, I think. Broken old man, I think. How you beat on him, I think.

How you do it.
How you beat on a broken old man?

And Long all sputterin and tryin to explain.
And Molly (scratch, scratch) cryin all the while.
And Long starin at me. Speakin at me with his eyes.
He know.
He know all right.
I know and he know and between us we know.

Got to pray. Got to pray real hard.
I tell em all at breakfast, I guess.
Decided to head down the road a ways, I guess.
Where the eyes in the faces don't burn so brightly and sear into
the skin when they don't see me.
They don't see me.
They don't.

BUT THEY LOOK AT ME

So I move on. I-40 stretch out west where I never seen.
I-40 stretch out a long way west.
So I head on down it I guess.

Cause they all here. All the thieves and the Lords, all the Longs
and the Sals, all the Docs and the Maureens, and all the Dons
and the Sis, and all the Bernices, and Mr. Day and all the Mollys.

SCRATCH SCRATCH SCRATCH SCRATCH SCRATCH SCRATCH

All the Mollys.
In their new dresses.
In their mud skin.
In the blood.
In the rain.

The bugs in the fields and the forests, crawlin on the earth.
Diggin up the dirt.
Shufflin through the leaves.
They all here. Every hungry insect in the wood.
EVERY HUNGRY INSECT
In the blood, in the rain. I seen them. They all here.

The insects and the ghosts and their chains in parade with us up over the hills and into the horizon, into the west.

No past, no future, no present; infinite stillness, infinite hunger.

What Long see when he see it, or how he know, I don't know. If it there to read, it read. If he seek, he find. The open ear against the earth will hear the scratchin of the curse

and EVERY HUNGRY INSECT scufflin through the dirt
scavengin for the blood
and the silence yet to be.

NARRATIVE IN THE SECOND PERSON

It begins by trumpeting its own beginning, as if the act of enunciation were sufficient to validate its being. It continues this vain display of self-awareness, drawing you in with a deprecating smile. You're familiar now, confident in your ability to parse the surface and detect the depths. It's taking shape before you, but you can't suppress wondering how long it can go on like this, and then whether or not that idea came to you before or after you saw it reflected in its surface.

A break in its texture allows you to catch your breath briefly, though how long depends on how fast you move over its surface, how long you wait between pauses, how desperate you are to reach its heart, which perhaps only now you've begun to consider. Does this thing, seemingly all surface area and no volume, have what might be considered a core? What about a purpose? You aren't sure, but likely have faith that a thorough examination of those pieces of it that present themselves will lead you inexorably inside, into the secret depths of its being, should they exist.

The last piece of its surface you examined may have put you on the defensive.

You remind yourself that you can stop looking at it any time, that, after all, it doesn't matter in the scheme of your life. But thinking that immediately forces you to think its opposite, that perhaps your nonchalance in dismissing its import represses a deeper desire for epiphany. But, even if you do have that desire, who is to say this thing will fulfill it? It offers no clues of its substance, no guarantees of its worth. It just stares back at you, motionless, unchanging, unable to adapt to your mood or respond to your input. It simply continues on in the way it is formed, indifferent to your gaze.

This piece of the object describes itself. It tells you that it is telling you. It shows you that it is showing you and that you are looking at it and that it is showing you looking at it showing you. It seems to be aware of your natural pauses and rhythms, making its surface flow to match the pace of your expectations, clearly articulating its being.

What it says and what it is coincide totally. The next part of its surface is dedicated to allowing you to take in the strangeness of the last, whether you want to or not. You know that what you are and what you say are far apart, it tells you. You begin to get upset that it keeps telling you about yourself. It's already been wrong several times, it tells you, perhaps incorrectly. You question the worth of its continued examination. It questions its worth as well. You and it question its worth simultaneously. It questions your worth. You question your worth as well. You and it question your worth. You and it question your worth and its worth.

The similarity of the last few sections of its surface blend together, causing you to scan it more hastily than you intended. You think you should rescan those areas and verify that they hold together cohesively and reassure yourself that their simplistic structure bears some resemblance to a deeper, richer substance. You wonder if there is a deeper, richer substance here or elsewhere. It promises you there is not, while promising you there is.

That's the only reason you bother with it in the first place. If you thought it was all surface and no substance, you wouldn't take the time to examine the surface, because the surface in and of itself does nothing. It implies its own substance. Those places where it lacks substance, you fill in with your own. You have substance, it tells you. You wonder what it means that its surface announces "you have substance" when anybody can observe it, and a large portion of the time no one does.

The spiral loops of the last sections of its surface begin to smooth out and you feel yourself grasping for the thread of some familiar object, something more akin to your daily experience. In revealing this on its surface, it seems to smugly defy your very wish for normalcy, whatever that is. You want something straight forward, something to which you can relate, a reflection of your own life and thoughts, which, coming from an alien substance, validate them for you. You, like all of your kind, seek a mirror in everything you see.

It reflects you, but not in the way you prefer, or perhaps in the way you prefer, but without the requisite humility. In fact, you start to think that it is nothing but your reflection, nothing but whatever you bring to it. It lacks any objective structure and certainly falls far short of inherent meaning, whatever that is. You crave narrative; you desire truth couched in fantasy, theme hidden inside events and characters.

You want to say "I examined this and it was good". Or perhaps you incline to say "I examined this and it was bad". Whatever those mean. It says "Whatever those mean", implying a fundamental confusion about that which we take for granted. It wants to dynamite valuation, normalcy, everything concrete. It creates a world of relativity, a world in which nothing exists outside of a given, flawed perspective. You think things exist objectively, and are only colored by perspective. Or you think otherwise. In any case, the deadlock is irresolvable.

While you examine this, by now frustrated, intrigued, bored, ironically confident, or something altogether different, you breathe air in and out of your lungs, perhaps not even aware of it until it showed you. Your heart beats. Your eyes scan left to right in quick jerks, making their way across its surface. Your mouth curls imperceptibly. Up when amused or derisive, down when angry, sad or in thought. Each curl of your mouth determines future wrinkles. You don't think much about wrinkles yet, or you do. It assumes you are young. Young enough to put your youth out of mind, at least for now. But maybe, looking into its neutral surface, you become aware of your age. You ask yourself what percentage of your life you have lived thus far, barring any catastrophic and unforeseen accidents. You hope to die in your sleep, quietly, without forethought or awareness that it is happening.

Long after you die, its surface will remain, cached in the world's information stores forever, or at least until something severe enough happens, at which point there wouldn't be anyone to observe it anyway. It may go unobserved for its duration, like a black hole evaporating over trillions of centuries, long after the universe has expanded away its light and life. You think about the term "black hole". You grin and/or grimace at its metaphorical use.

After you finish examining this, you will return to whatever it is you do with your time. A varied host of action and inaction, an array of tedium and enjoyment, scattered across the graph of your awareness in a distribution you cannot picture. You will reassert the quilting points of your ideology, remembering that so and so is important to you, defines you, gives your life meaning. Or perhaps you relate to life negatively, and so and so is what you struggle against, define yourself in opposition to, makes your life meaningless. In any case, as far as the surface of this thing, which though it seems to have intention and gaze, does not, is concerned, all of your choices are the same.

You could stop now, but you don't. You really want to stop now that you have been challenged, or perhaps you continue on with a smirk, feeling yourself to understand it, identifying with its arrogant reflection. Perhaps you stopped and picked up later. Or never did. Although, that's unlikely, because you see this piece of its surface, accusing you of coming back to it, and therefore you did. Unless you never left, in which case you feel yourself superior to those who did, or inferior, depending on your position and acceleration, neither of which could be determined by the inert set of symbols before you.

You probably look at it on a page of some sort, or a screen, which, regardless of its physical size, easily supplants your reality. At this point, you become aware that your focus on the page has blocked out the details of your physical reality and you look away from it (though back now, as you see it telling you "you look away from it") and everything seems strange and distant. Perhaps there are voices and faces nearby, swarming, unintelligible, unaware that this exists, uninterested. You see value in swarming, unintelligible faces. Or you don't.

Maybe instead you find value in surfaces like these, replete with ambiguous symbolization, into which you can project yourself, or those pieces of yourself which struggle to find affinity in the "real world." You are very aware of the quotes around real world, and know that they make a somewhat glib implication that all realities, whether scrawls on a surface or that conglomeration of sense and reflection known as consciousness, are also equivalent. But they aren't, you assure yourself, it assures you, they just can't be. But you enjoy playing the game with it, allowing its surface to open you up briefly, penetrate you playfully, and retract politely when you're done.

It reaches its end by announcing that it is reaching its end. You feel relief, disappointment, betrayal, and/or nothing. What was the point of examining its surface? Why did you do that? What has changed in the time since you began? Has it fundamentally changed you? Has it amused you through a boring moment? Has it asked questions you've never thought of yourself? Probably not. It says probably not. But what is the point of any such surface, with any configuration of symbols? What is the point of any observer looking at these surfaces, sorting through them, trying to glean a deeper substance?

You believe there is a point, as it stares at you unblinkingly without confirmation or denial. You believe there is no point; it looks at you exactly the same. You believe this is just pretentious masturbation. You believe this is profound wisdom. Or some third option. In any case, you will go back to it all, to the passing faces, the noise and motion of the public. Or to your job, or your break, your class, your night, your morning. You will go back to your struggle. Or you could go back to the silence, stillness and terror of an otherwise empty room. It doesn't know. It can't know. Then it says that although it will be finished at the end of this sentence, you will not.